Also by Ken Bruen,
published by The Do-Not Press:
The Hackman Blues
The White Trilogy:
A White Arrest
Taming The Alien
The McDead
London Boulevard
Blitz

Other books by Ken Bruen:
Funeral
Shades of Grace
Martyrs
Rilke on Black
Her Last Call to Louis McNeice
The Guards
The Killing of the Tinkers
The Magdalen Martyrs

D0365994

1

KEN BRUEN
VIXEN

Ken Bruen.

THE DO-NOT PRESS

First Published in Great Britain in 2003 by
The Do-Not Press Ltd
16 The Woodlands
London SE13 6TY
www.thedonotpress.com
email: vixen@thedonotpress.com

B-format paperback: ISBN 1 904316-31-X
Casebound edition: ISBN 1 904316-30-1

British Library Cataloguing in Publication Data. A catalogue
record for this book is available from the British Library.

b   d   f   h   g   e   c   a

Printed and bound in Great Britain

FOR PAT MULLAN

AND

KT MCCAFFREY

THRILLER AND CRIME WRITERS OF THE FIRST RANK.

1

SERGEANT DOYLE HAD his feet up on a stool. The station was quiet and he wasn't anticipating trouble. Football was on the telly so the hordes would be indoors. He'd nicked a danish from the canteen and had been looking forward to it all day.

He opened *The Sun* and was about to bite into the danish when the phone rang. He took a fast chomp and picked up. A man's voice said:

'Might I suggest you tape this call?'

'All calls are taped as a matter of form.'

A piece of the pastry had lodged in his bad back tooth and he used a finger to try and move it. The man said:

'I don't feel I have your full attention.'

Doyle sighed and said:

'I'm fascinated, trust me.'

'You will be. A bomb is due to go off in... three minutes.

This is not really a warning, more of a wake-up call. Do you know the Paradise Cinema?'

'Off Waterloo Avenue? Is that where the bomb is?'

A loud bang went off in Doyle's ear and he instinctively pushed the phone away. When the noise had subsided he asked:

'Was that it?'

He heard a low chuckle, then:

'Whoops, the timing was a little off but we'll be working on that. What you have to work on is getting three hundred grand together to make sure we don't bomb again. I mean, that's not a huge amount, is it? So you get started on that and we'll try not to blow up anything else in the meantime. We'll give you a bell tomorrow and see how you're progressing. Oh, and in case you're wondering, the movie playing at the Paradise was a Tom Cruise piece of shit so we kind of did the public a service. You be good now.'

Click.

Doyle kept the phone his ear, clicked the connection and set about alerting the necessary departments. The pastry had already caused his tooth to hum and he said aloud:

'Oh fuck.'

The Paradise Cinema was a recent addition to the area's cultural landscape. It catered largely to local residents and usually attracted a respectable crowd. The bomb had been placed in one of the toilets and nobody had been hurt.

Panic and fear had spread quickly and the crowd had piled into the street, pushing and shoving each other, afraid that another bomb could go off. The Bomb Squad arrived and cordoned off the street. Superintendent Brown was on the scene, ordering officers to hold back the crowd.

He shouted at Chief Inspector Roberts to get every available man out canvassing the area and see if anybody knew anything or had seen anything. He asked:

'Where's Porter Nash and that crony of yours, Brant? Where's he when he's wanted?'

Roberts had no idea and said:

'I've no idea.'

'Some bloody copper you are. This better not be terrorists.'

'I don't think so, sir. The tape asked for money. I think it's straightforward extortion.'

Brown looked like he'd have a coronary and ranted:

'Straightforward? When the bloody hell was extortion straightforward?'

Roberts wanted to shout back, *you stupid prick, you know what I mean,* but settled for:

'I don't think it's an international deal.'

'That puts all our minds at rest, then – the great detective has spoken.'

The Bomb Squad commander came out of the cinema and Roberts was saved from having to reply. Brown asked him:

'What have we got?

The bomb guy said:

'You're talking bottom of the barrel here.'

Brown took a deep breath, asked the Grand Designer of the Masons for patience, said:

'Could you put that in words I might understand?'

The bomb guy exchanged a look with Roberts that said:

'This asshole's your boss, you got my sympathy, pal.'

Out loud he said:

'Couldn't be simpler, two sticks of dynamite and a cheap timer. Any idiot could put it together.'

Brown was staring at Roberts' shoes. They were heavy brown Oxfords with a high sheen. Two questions came into his head:

How did he afford them?

and

Who'd the time to polish shoes to such a degree?

Pulling his eyes back to the bomb guy, he asked:

'Any idea who the idiot could be?'

'Stick a pin in the phone book.'

'That's a fucking help all right.'

A smile from the bomb guy and he was gone. Brown turned to Roberts, asked,

'Where did you get those shoes?'

'What?'

'Are you deaf?'

'Oh, right... ahm, at a sale, at Bally.'

'Bally!' Then: 'How the hell can you afford them?'

'The house was sold.'

'That's an answer?'

'The only one I've got.'

Brown gave the shoes a last look, then:

'I expect a report on my desk tomorrow morning and keep Brant away from it.'

He strode off, muttering darkly. Roberts was tempted to shout 'God Bless' but knew it would be pushing it.

PC Falls had yet again failed the sergeant's exam. She didn't take it well, said:

'Fucking racist bastards.'

Porter Nash, recently promoted to detective inspector, approached, tried:

'Next time, eh, for sure?'

Falls was the wet dream of the nick but over the last year, she'd acquired a fearsome rep. Despite her pretty face, athletic body, the guys were avoiding her. A rumour had circulated she might have offed a cop killer.

Not a clean offing.

No, the guy had been literally hammered to bits. The Forensics team had found body parts all over the room. His nose was stuck to a widescreen TV. Well, part of the septum at any rate. What they finally decided had to be his left eye was floating in the toilet bowl. Teeth were strewn across the wide bed. When word of the butchery leaked, the possible culprit was definitely assumed to be a cop.

In the frame were:

Of course... Brant. He topped the list of any wrong doing: he was your 'given'. No decent odds ever on him.

Next, as a rank outsider, was Porter Nash because in his

Kensington days, he'd dished out personal justice to a pae-
dophile.

Falls was not seriously considered at first but, over
time, speculation and rumour had moved her to top of the
list.

Number one with a bullet.

Sergeant Brant had long been the *bête noire* of south-
east London. Villains and cops alike were united in their
fear of him. He relished and encouraged his status as 'an
animal'. The accidental death of the Clapham Rapist was
attributed to him. This outlaw justice was secretly admired
by most ranks. Over the years Superintendent Brown had
tried unsuccessfully to get rid of him. Despite his disappointment, the senior officer still cherished dreams of
discrediting the sergeant.

Falls, turning on Porter, put her hands on her hips, tried
to bite down her bile but it wasn't working. She spat:

'Next time? You condescending prick, have you any
idea how often I've sat that bloody exam?'

Porter glanced round nervously; the other cops were
getting an earful and hoping for more. He put his hand
out, touched her shoulder, said:

'Let me get you some tea.'

She stormed off and Porter, at a loss, stared at her back.
The desk sergeant, an obnoxious bollix, gave him the
thumbs up. Porter sighed and took off, just in time to see
her disappear into the Cricketers pub. When he entered,
Falls was already at a corner table. He approached, asked:

'What'll you have?'

'I'm getting it. I ordered for you too.'

Porter looked towards the barman. He thought he imagined it but did the guy wink? Jesus.

Porter sat down and Falls asked:

'You still smoking or has your promotion put a stop to simple pleasures?'

He reached into his jacket – a smart leather job from Gap – and placed a green pack on the table. Falls snorted, said:

'Fucking menthol! How gay is that?'

She extracted one, smelled it, managing to add a note of sensuality to the gesture, then snapped her fingers, said:

'Light.'

He wanted to reach over, smack her in the mouth but suppressed it, fired her up. She did that annoying thing women do, took two drags, stubbed it out. Well, stabbed it twice in the ashtray, leaving it to smoulder. He reached over, burnt his fingers as he tried to extinguish the glow. He saw a flicker of a smile touch her lips. The barman breezed over, a tray held aloft, a riot of crisps and peanuts on it. Falls asked:

'What's the deal on the snacks? I didn't order them.'

Chuckle from the barman, he nodded towards Porter, said:

'Experience, darlin'. Been as long in this game as I have, you know your punter who's going to want his salt 'n' vinegar. This way I save a trip.'

Falls took the glasses, handed one to Porter, said:

'He'll need paying.'

It was twice what Porter would have guessed; he didn't figure on much return from his twenty. The barman was back at the bar when Falls shouted:

'Pack of B&H.'

Got the look.

Porter sniffed his drink, asked:

'Vodka? At those prices, they must be doubles.'

She nodded and took a hefty slug, Porter couldn't drink it neat and shouted towards the bar:

'Bottle of tonic… slimline.'

When the barman sniggered, Porter realised he was sounding like Arthur Daley which would never be a good idea. When the tonic and cigs came, the barman glared at Porter. As he left, Porter asked:

'What was that about?'

Falls was opening peanuts, said:

'He's homophobic.'

'Ah, come on, you're saying he knows I'm gay?'

Falls eyed him and, with little affection, a shard of granite across her pupils, said:

'Everybody knows.'

He let it slide. There'd been a time when he and Falls had been best mates. Almost from the off, they'd bonded, went dancing, drinking together. Then she'd bought into a shitpile of trouble. A skinhead she'd been friendly with was murdered and her life began to spiral. Porter's promotion had sealed their separation. He was worried by the speed of her drinking. Her trouble with the booze had definitely worked against her attempt at sergeant. He asked:

'How are you and Nelson doing?'

This was a detective from Vauxhall who'd saved Falls' job then had begun a relationship with her. Porter had only met him a few times and found him to be aggressive and worse, dull. Vital qualifications for the Met. She signalled for another round then answered:

'Nelson? Nelson is history.'

'I'm sorry.'

She let her face show major surprise, gasped:

'Oh, you knew him?'

'Not really.'

Now her lip curled and she snarled:

'Then why the fuck are you sorry? For all you know, I'm well shot of him.'

Porter stood up, shrugged his shoulders

'I'll leave you to it.'

A young cop came in, saw them and came over, said:

'Sir, you're wanted, it's the bombing.'

Porter looked at Falls, asked:

'Coming?'

'I'm getting bombed here. You run along, do senior officer stuff.'

Some find themselves through joy, some through suffering and some through toil. Johnny had till now tried nothing but whiskey. A process that left him feeling like somebody new every day.'

Nelson Algren, *The Man With The Golden Arm*.

2

ANGIE JAMES WAS seriously deranged. She'd learnt that early and just as quickly had learnt to hide it. Took her a while to grasp that other people had a sense of right and wrong. Her radar operated on feeling good or feeling cheated. There was little in between. Imitation was her salvation, miming what others expressed honed her survival skills.

But at a cost.

Attempting to incinerate her family as a teenager got her a two-year spell in a psychiatric unit. The best two years she'd had as she'd discovered the power of sex.

And what a dizzying power it was.

Her face was pretty in an unremarkable way. Make-up made you notice. Long afternoons with fashion mags taught her how to shape and hone her body to the level of desirability. Clothes added the rest. Going before the review board, she'd learnt enough to feed them the responses they wanted.

At the age of 28, she'd only made one serious error in the intervening years. One night in a pub, she'd opened a guys face – from the left eyebrow to the chin – with an open razor. Not because she was angry but from a vague interest in seeing his reaction. She did a year in Holloway where she seriously maimed a bull dyke.

For her time there, she was celling with a woman in her fifties named Beth, doing ten to fifteen for a string of post office heists. In a prison dispute Angie had waded in and saved her from a serious beating, purely out of boredom. Beth was grateful, lent her books, cosmetics, cigarettes. One stiflingly hot July day, she'd said:

'Angie, you should be set up for life, you know that?'

Angie didn't answer, busy with a *Cosmo* quiz.

'I'm serious, hon, get yourself a stash, head for Florida, marry one of the rich fucks there, hump him to a heart attack.'

'How do I get the stash?'

Beth was a bit drunk, on prison hooch. It tasted like rot-gut but got you there and fast. She wanted Angie to have the dream she'd never achieved, said:

'There's only one sure crime, pays big with little risk and you do it right, you're set.'

Angie had moved on to an article telling how to give better oral sex, asked:

'What's the crime?'

Beth took another swig of the booze, tried to focus, said:

'Extortion.'

'Yeah, and that works how?'

Beth had to lie down, the brew was packing a wallop like a baton. She completely lost her train of thought, was even finding it difficult to remember who the hell Angie was. But Angie was finally interested, pushed:

'Come on, girl, what's the deal?'

Gradually and painfully, she learnt the master plan. Bomb a building then demand a payment not to bomb any more. Angie sneered:

'That's it, that's the answer? It's fucked is what it is.'

Beth had passed out.

Six months after Angie's release, Beth was blinded by a dodgy batch of brew. Even if Angie had written, as she'd promised she'd do but didn't, Beth couldn't have read the letters.

Angie was seeing two brothers, Ray and Jimmy Cross. Ray was the brains and Jimmy the muscle. Small-time operators, they were crazy about her. That she serviced both didn't bother either of them. Their main attraction was a Mews they rented off the Clapham Road. It was crammed with hot DVDs, laptops, bogus designer label fashion. They'd been eating curry, chugging Special Brew and vaguely watching *Dumb and Dumber*.

Jimmy said:

'I found some dynamite today.'

Ray threw a can at him, said:

'You stupid fuck, how are we going to flog that?'

Angie sat up, asked:

'Where did you find it?'

Delighted to have her attention, Jimmy rushed:

'We was doing a spliff in that old house on Meadow Road, I pulled a tarpaulin aside and there it was, a crate of the stuff.'

Ray opened a fresh Special, shouted:

'Get rid, you hear.'

Angie was up

'No, no, I've an idea.'

3

BRANT WENT:

'Ahh...'

The hooker finished up, wiped her mouth and got to her feet. Brant stretched, said:

'There's brewskis in the fridge, grab us two.'

She glared at him, wanted to shout:

'Get them yourself, yer fucking pig!'

But she'd known him longer than she wanted to remember, went to the kitchen, rinsed her mouth, spat, said:

'Good riddance.'

There was a small mirror over the sink and she checked her face. The reflection told the harsh truth: a tired hooker with way too much mileage, the lines of twenty years and all of them hard. Brant from the other room:

'What, you brewing them? Get your tush in here.'

She grabbed the beers and headed back. He'd put on his trousers, which was a relief, and he tapped the coffee table, said:

'Plant them here, babe.'

She stared at the table, apparently lost. He asked:

'You deaf? Plonk them on here.'

'You don't have coasters?'

He leant over, grabbed a can, popped the tab, gulped half, belched, said:

'If you're not having that, slide it on over.'

She pulled the top, took a ladylike sip. This amused him and he asked:

'Teach you that at finishing school?'

She looked at him, said:

'Yeah, the Mile End Road. They're real big on etiquette.'

He finished the beer, crushed the can and lobbed it over his shoulder, asked:

'Got any smokes?'

She tried not to sigh, got her handbag, threw over a pack. He caught it, cursed.

'Silk Cut? The fuck are those?'

''Cos of my chest.'

He tore off the filter, said:

'You standing there? Light me up.'

The phone rang. Brant reached over, grabbed it, said:

'Yo?'

'Brant, it's Roberts, we've got a situation.'

Brant winked at the hooker, said:

'Just had me a situation, too.'

'I don't doubt it. Can you get down here?'

'On my way.'

He stood up, stretched, and the hooker asked:

'How long have we known each other?'

'Whoa… who's counting?'

'So, did I ever ask you for anything? Not once, not even a few quid?'

He mimed horror, said:

'You mean you were faking, it wasn't love?'

'There's a guy, name of Millovitz, some European geezer, he's been beating the girls at the Oval, says they'll get hurt bad if they don't pay him weekly. One of the girls, he broke her nose and in this game, that drives value way down.'

Brant selected a pair of tan cords and sparkling white shirt, pulled out a stolen police federation tie, did it up in a Windsor knot. He sat, pulled on heavy work boots then selected a short black raincoat. The wardrobe was open and she could see a ton of new clothes, still with tags on. She could see they were designer labels and what they said to her was money, lots of money. Brant smiled, said:

'Fell off a lorry, know what I mean?'

She didn't answer, Brant did a twirl, asked:

'What do you think? See me on the street, would you get hot?'

She thought she'd get the hell away – everything about him screamed cop. She gave a weak smile, Brant reached down, touched his toes, said:

'Listen.'

He rapped his knuckle and a dull zing sounded. Straightening, he said:

'Steel caps. So what time does this shithead usually make an appearance?'

4

AROUND THE TABLE were Porter Nash, PC McDonald, Brant, assorted plain-clothes officers and, at the top, Chief Inspector Roberts. One of the detectives asked:

'What's the PC doing here?'

Roberts looked to Brant who gave a lazy smile, said:

'You'll be wanting tea, coffee… '

The guy unsure, glanced round for help, none was forthcoming so he said:

'Yes, sure… 'course.'

Brant nodded at McDonald, said:

'There's your tea-boy.'

A round of sniggers and McDonald glared at Brant who winked. Roberts coughed, then:

'Okay, settle down. We've got a bomber and according to the Bomb Squad, we're dealing with an amateur. Which is not to say people might not get hurt. In fact, with them, it's more dangerous than professionals as they don't know what they're doing. I want blanket door-to-door inter-views, computer printout of any individual with any connection to dynamite or blasting, enquiries to building sites to see if any explosive's been stolen. Get out on the street, get me something. Any questions?'

Porter put up his hand, asked:

'What's the deal on the money demand?'

'There's no deal. The Super says no payment.'

Porter raised his eyebrows, said:

'Then we can expect another blast.'

'Not if we catch them first, okay? Now let's get moving. Sergeant Brant, a word please.'

As they filed out, Brant said to McDonald:

'Mug of tea, two sugars… oh, and a wedge of danish… that's a good boy.'

After they'd gone, Roberts shut the door, said:

'The Super doesn't want you in on this.'

Brant looked round the room, studied the range of 'No Smoking' signs then pulled out his Weights, fired up, blew a cloud at them, answered:

'So, what else is new?'

'She hoped he was burning in hell. What she'd done, she'd done for Loretta and for the sake of having a little fun, a pretty scarce commodity for a woman with a small child and no husband.
She wasn't sorry for any of it. Not for one goddamn minute of it.
Scott Phillips, *The Walkaway*.

5

FALLS HAD HAD a shitty day.

As regards the bomber, which was currently A-list, she was out of the loop. Her past connections to the principals – Brant, Roberts, Porter Nash – hadn't cut any ice. Even the mundane crap, the bottom-feeder stuff, like the door-to-door slog, didn't include her.

She'd managed to catch Roberts alone in the canteen, a rare moment for the man heading up the hunt and asked:

'Join you for a sec, guv?'

He hadn't quite rebuffed her but it was in the neighbourhood, said:

'I don't have a whole load of time.'

She wanted to shout:

'You shithead, when your wife died and you climbed

into a vat of red wine, who pulled you out… who had a whole lot of time then?'

But went with:

'I won't keep you, sir.'

As she sat, he glanced at his watch. There are many ways to say *Hey, you're no longer a player* but this has the benefit of being the shortest. You also get to see the time. Nervous, she almost unconsciously reached for her smokes and he asked:

'You're not thinking of smoking are you, not into my face?'

Closed her bag, said:

''Course not, sir.'

Wondering when exactly he'd made the leap to complete prick. Worse, he was tapping the fingers of his right hand on the table and snapped:

'What is it, Falls? I'm not a mind reader.'

'Ahm, yes… right, I was wondering… if I might, er, help in the current investigation?'

He stared at her, appeared truly astonished, said:

'Don't you know you're under a cloud? I mean, surely you realise your very job is hanging by a thread?'

'I thought, sir, that… thought all that was behind me.'

He stood up, straightened his tie, ran his fingers through his hair and without looking at her, said:

'You thought wrong.'

And was gone.

6

BRANT CHECKED HIS watch: ten after ten. He was
parked about a hundred yards from the Oval tube in a side
road to the left of St Mark's Church. During the day, a
drinking school holds sway. Bottles of 'white lady' are the
drink, if not of choice, definitely of necessity. Usually pure
methylated spirit, sometimes it's spiked with cider. Get a
blend of tastes going. Come night, the hookers set up shop
and a steady stream of cars cruise the patch. Though not
on the scale of King's Cross, it's a steady enterprise.

Brant clocked the makes of cars, almost all in good condition. Not hurting for cash but obviously lacking in
balance. Few things as hazardous as street sex and not just
the risk of diseases but, he supposed, it all added to the
rush.

Around eleven, a van pulled up, parked on the kerb. A

white van, not unlike the one every American law enforcement agency was looking for in the Washington sniper case a few years back. A tall blond guy wearing a cream leather jacket (to accessorise the van?) and black combat pants climbed out. His hair thick and long, poured over his upturned collar. Brant muttered:

'General fucking Custer.'

The guy's back was pumped, muscles showing through the leather: steroids and gym, the new addiction. He approached the hookers, said a few words then backhanded one. Another started to shout and he punched her in the stomach. Brant reached for a tyre iron, paused, saying, 'Naw...' and let it be. He got out and slammed his car door but if the guy heard, he didn't care. Brant was delighted, he loved the stupid ones.

The guy was raising his hands again and Brant shouted: 'Yo, Custer?'

The guy turned, in no hurry. Whatever was coming, he could deal with it. He looked at Brant, asked:

'You calling me, prick-face?'

Brant smiled, this was better than he'd hoped. Moved to within a cigarette of the guy, said:

'I'm Sergeant Brant. Due to recent public concern, we have to identify ourselves from the off. My name mean anything to you?'

The guy dredged up phlegm from deep in his chest, sampled it, then brought it up, letting his head back, he hawked the full load, then spat it to an inch of Brant's left shoe, said:

'That name don't mean shit to me.'

Brant didn't move, which set off an alarm in the guy's confidence.

Brant said:

'Oh, that's not very nice. Watch out, she's behind you.'

Almost never failed, the oldest ruse in the book and the shitheads went for it every time. The guy turned and Brant hit him with the low kidney shot, felling him like a sack of Galway potatoes. He moved round then with the steel caps, delivered a staccato of kicks to the body. A small cheer went up from the girls. Brant hunkered down, grabbed the blond hair with his left hand and dragged the guy's face up, said:

'You gotta be hurting, am I right?... No, no, don't answer 'cos I still have to break your nose... shshhhhhh, be done before you can shout "police intimidation".'

And it was.

Brant straightened up, reached for his cigs, fired up, finally turned to the hookers who were gaping at him. No strangers to violence, they were stunned at the casual ferocity. Brant gave his wolf smile, said:

'Nice evening for it.'

Then nudging the guy with the tip of his shoe, he said:

'I see you again, you're history.'

As he got back in the car, he enjoyed the sight of the women rolling the guy.

Falls wanted a drink; she wanted a lot of drinks. The Roebuck was usually quiet midweek and on her way to the bar she clocked a few lone drinkers. A surly barman slapped her drink on the counter. She was preparing to have his ass when a customer banged into her, said:

'Sorry, lost my balance.'

And he veered away, heading for the door. A young woman rose from a table, grabbed him and got his arm midway on his back, put her hand in his pocket then shoved him away, snarling

'Now, fuck off.'

He made for the door and was gone. The woman walked to Falls, held out a purse, said:

'He dipped you.'

Falls stared at her purse in astonishment, thinking, *I never felt him*, then asked:

'Can I buy you a drink? It's the very least I can do.'

The woman, blonde, pretty, in expensive clothes gave a radiant smile, said:

'Sure, large vodka, loads of ice.'

Falls signalled to the barman, asked her:

'Just ice?'

'Yeah, why fuck it up?'

Falls liked her already. They moved to a table and Falls raised her glass, said:

'Thanks so much.'

She said, 'No big thing,' and sank the double like a docker, raised her finger, said:

'Yo, bar-person. Hit us again.'

Then she produced a pack of Rothmans, asked:

'Hope you don't mind?'

Falls couldn't believe she'd found a kindred spirit, put out her hand, went:

'I'm Elizabeth.'

And was amazed with herself as she never normally gave her first name.

The woman took her hand, said:

'I'm happy to meet you.'

After another round, Falls was seriously wrecked, said:

'I'm a cop.'

'Yeah?'

Not interested, cool about it. Falls continued:

'And I've got to say you handled that guy like you were a cop yourself.'

The woman flashed the smile, said:

'I work the clubs. Bit of dancing, some hostessing, and a whole pile of assholes.'

Falls got out some paper, wrote her number down, said:

'Listen, let's get together again, my treat.'

The woman nodded and glanced at her watch, said:

'Got to run.'

Falls went to stand, staggered, then:

'I don't even know your name.'

Over her shoulder, as she left, the woman said:

'Angie.'

A car was parked up the street and Angie got in, the two brothers waiting. One asked:

'How did it go?'

'Piece of cake, she's a lush.'

Ray, the smart one, asked:

'Why did you have to be so rough when you grabbed me?'

'Make it look real. She's a cop, she'd smell a bogus stunt.'

Jimmy, the muscle, asked:

'What do you want to meet a cop for?'

Angie tapped her forehead, said:

'We want to know how the investigation is going, who better to tell us than a cop?'

Ray, negotiating traffic, was shaking his head, went:

'Seems risky to me.'

''Course it's risky, that's the fucking rush.'

7

THE SECOND EXPLOSION was at a teenage disco, situated off Coldharbour Lane. A large hall had been converted by local builders, its aim to keep teenagers away from the main strip in Brixton. So now the kids hit the strip first, scored the dope, then went to the disco. Parents, delighted at the lack of booze, congratulated themselves on their efforts.

Two parents, acting as bouncers, were injured in the blast. The dynamite had been placed in a litter bin sited conveniently at the main entrance. The victims, covered in blood, were on the front page of all the papers with screaming headlines:

BOMBER TARGETS TEENS

Roberts, all control gone, was shouting:

'They didn't phone... why didn't they bloody phone? I

mean, play fucking fair, we never even got a chance to answer the ransom demand. What the hell is going on?'

No one knew. Roberts glared at his team. Porter Nash, clearing his throat, began:

'I met with the Bomb Squad.'

'Yeah?'

'It's the same outfit, same MO. A few sticks of dynamite and the crude timer.'

Brant, lit a cig, exhaled, asked:

'Any luck on the usual suspects?'

'No, seems to be a new operator.'

Roberts slammed his hand on the table, said:

'I've to meet the Super in ten minutes... is that what I tell him... ? That we figure it's a new operator? He's going to fucking lap that up, bound to be commendations all round.'

Porter Nash felt he should say something further, tried:

'The victims are doing well, the injuries looked worse than they actually were.'

Roberts wasn't placated

'Take a look at the bloody tabloids, the damage is already done.'

A silence descended and the atmosphere was thick with recrimination.

The phone rang.

'I ran a tape I'd rented on the way back, Jennifer Jason Leigh in *Rush*. I felt like watching cops get fucked up.'
Matthew Stokoe, *High Life*

8

ROBERTS GRABBED THE phone, said:

'Yes?'

A robotic tone, speaking through one of those voice-changers, asked:

'You in charge of the bomber case?'

'Yes, I'm Chief Inspector Roberts.'

'Impressive title, you like to use that, I'd say. What you'd do, kiss some major ass to get there?'

'Is that a question?'

Heard a snigger, someone in the background, then:

'Naw, I like fucking with you. Lighten up, pal, these are the jokes. You'll have had a second explosion?'

Roberts was furious, he felt chest pains, asked:

'What happened to a warning? What happened to you calling about the money?'

More sniggers, then:

'Tell you the truth, Rob, it got away from us. That ever happen to you? The truth is, we changed the rules. You want to know why?'

'Why?'

''Cos we can.'

Roberts glanced round the room, saw the stone expressions, said:

'You want payment, you'll have to play by some rules.'

Silence and he thought the call had ended, then a harsher tone:

'You fuck-face, you mind if I call you that? Not that it matters, you're a messenger boy, got it? Your function is to act as bagman. We want six large.'

'What?'

'Two explosions – this shit is expensive. Time and money, you get my meaning? But hey, I can lighten up, cut you some slack. How would it be if I give you 48 hours, say Friday evening, round 6.00? I'll give you a bell, that help at all?'

Roberts took a deep breath, tried to rein in his rage, said:

'I'll need more time.'

'No can do, fellah.'

Click.

Roberts put the phone down, said:

'See if there's any hope of a trace. Not that I expect one.'

No trace.

9

FALLS CAME TO with a bad hangover. She was wearing a long old Snoopy T-shirt that had been washed so often the dog was no longer distinguishable. Her mouth was like a desert and she went to the kitchen, gulped a glass of water. It hit her stomach like ice and she retched, said:

'That's it, I'm never drinking again, least not on week nights.'

This was a familiar mantra: as comfortable as it was bogus. She began to boil some water, thinking tea would help, at least wake her up.

She was up for a new assignment. Word was that a new WPC was coming on board and Falls would be nurse-maiding her. Of all the duties she loathed, this was the one she loathed most. All that enthusiasm, the high ideals and the spirit of camaraderie they expected. It was so fucking wearing. Then came the gradual erosion of energy and an initial disbelief that developed into full-blown cynicism. When they asked with that bright, fresh tone: '*What am I to do?*' Falls longed to scream: 'QUIT!'

Yeah, like they were ever going to believe her. Then Brant would come sniffing as he always did with the new ones and he'd turn on the full Celtic charm. Few could charm like that devil. She'd succumbed herself and more than once. He'd fuck them over every which way till Tuesday and they'd come back for more.

She dressed in her uniform and stood back to survey what she saw. *A black woman dressed in the clothes of the enemy*, that's what a black man had told her in Brixton market. She'd tried to rationalise it, told him that at least this way they had help in the ranks, knew how weak she sounded and saw his lip curl with disdain. He rapped:

'Yo be fooling your own self, girl.'

More and more, she was coming to believe he had been right. Using a brush, she flicked flecks of white off the tunic, and ran a hand through her frizzy hair. Once, in a moment of madness, she'd had all the kinks ironed out and that had hurt like a son-of-a-bitch.

Rosie had been alive then and when she'd seen the result, she'd wailed:

'Oh, big mistake! Are you trying to pass for white?'

That hurt and in more ways than she'd ever admit. Rosie had been her best friend, a WPC on the ladder up. They'd called themselves the poor man's Cagney and Lacey, and had shared the chauvinism they'd had to endure on a daily basis. Then one day Rosie had gone on a routine call, a domestic, hardly even worth writing up. The guy, a junkie with Aids, had bitten her. Tormented as to how she'd tell her husband, she'd slit her wrists and taken a long, hot bath; was dead before the water went cold. Falls had sworn then that she'd never get close to another cop, it was too risky.

She arrived early at the station and at the door, a fresh faced young woman in uniform eagerly approached, asking, 'WPC Flass?'

Falls sighed, said:

'You're going to be a policewoman?'

'Oh, yes.'

'Then take the bloody time to get my name right.'

The woman was in those impossible early twenties, where they look barely sixteen. She had black hair cut short, brown eyes and a face that might have been described as pretty if you had three drinks behind you. The uniform disguised her shape but she seemed to be in good physical nick. It was the fresh-faced energy that annoyed Falls, the gung-ho, raring- to-go shit that they presented. Falls asked:

'How did you know it was me?'

The woman looked back towards the desk sergeant, who was grinning from ear to ear, hesitated, and Falls said:

'Spit it out, he told you to wait for the nigger, is that it? You want to work with me, you better get honest; I can't stand lies.'

This was a little rich coming from Falls, who told lies all

the time, but what the hell? The thing with young people is they tend to believe outrageous crap like that. The woman gave an uncertain smile, said:

'He told me you'd be late... and that you'd be hung-over... oh, and that you were black as his shoe.'

Falls gave him the look, which he enjoyed immensely, the fuck even winked, and then she asked:

'What's your name?'

'WPC Andrews.'

The pride with which she trotted it out was appalling and, worse, you knew she'd rehearsed it a hundred times, probably in front of a mirror. She'd have a family, a happy mum and dad who were so proud of their little girl. All the frigging neighbours would have turned out to wish her well and they'd watch *The Bill* with renewed vigour. Falls gave her the fixed stare, said:

'One of the traits required of a police person is accuracy: an ability to actually listen to the question you are asked. Now let's try again: what is your name, not your flaming rank and serial number, can you do that?

She could and said:

'Patricia Andrews, but my friends call me Trish.'

This was much as Falls expected: stupidity and confidence, the worst combination there is. In jig time, of course, she'd be called Julie and every wag in the station would whistle 'The Sound of Music' at least once as she passed. Falls brushed past her, said:

'Let's get to the most important part of policing.'

Andrews was near gushing, went:

'We're going to get our assignment?'

'No, we're going to get tea.'

Falls led the way, a disappointed Andrews trailing behind. The canteen was full of uniformed officers who all turned to gawk at the new girl. Falls said:

'You'll need to know two things – the tea lady is named Gladys and the morons here call tea "a Sid Vicious" because in the movie *Sid and Nancy*, Gary Oldman tells his record exec to get a tea with two sugars and adds "Yah cunt".'

Andrews didn't understand this at all and Falls wasn't sure she did either. Falls took a table and Andrews asked:

'So do I ask Gladys for a Sid Vicious?'

'No, you ask for two teas and a Club Milk.'

Andrews lightened and asked:

'Oh, can I have a Club Milk too?'

'It's not for us, it's for Brant.'

As Andrews approached the counter she glanced back at Falls and that's when the bomb went off.

10

IT WAS A small blast, only damaging the counter and Gladys' nerves. But there was consternation in the canteen and men rushing for the exit. Brant appeared and moved quickly to the area, pulled Andrews clear, said:

'Get the fuck out, there might be a second.'

The station was evacuated and the Bomb Squad arrived, as did the press. Cops were piled three lines deep outside and within a half-hour, the all-clear was given and the canteen sealed off for Forensics. A mobile catering van was ordered as the cops couldn't – wouldn't – work without a steady stream of tea. Andrews, her uniform covered in dust, was highly excited and blabbering like an idiot till Falls, exasperated, slapped her face, said:

'Shut the fuck up. Jesus!'

She did.

Brant watching, gave a huge smile, said:

'Welcome to the Met.'

The bomb had been posted to the canteen and Gladys had left it until later. Roberts gathered his team and as they took their seats, the phone went. He picked up, heard the metallic voice:

'Sorry to interrupt your tea but this was a little incentive to get you up to speed. Remember the deadline, and now you know how vulnerable you are.'

Click.

Roberts looked round the room, said:

'The Super is going to throw a blue fit. Did anyone ever think to monitor the post?'

Nobody had. They went back to assessing the results so far and concluded they had nothing. Later, the Bomb Squad reported that the bomb was the same as the previous two but had been designed to frighten rather than maim.

Roberts sighed, said:

'Like that's going to save my ass.'

When he got to finally see the Super, he was dreading the bollocking he knew was coming. Brown was having his afternoon tea, a Kimberley biscuit on the saucer. Roberts knew from horrendous experience that the Super dunked the biscuit and then strained it between his teeth, making loud slurping sounds as he did so. It was on a par with Imelda Marcos singing 'Impossible Dream' or William Shatner's version of 'Bridge Over Troubled Waters'. If anything, it probably had the edge in grotesqueness. To Roberts' amazement, Brown was strangely subdued and the anticipated roaring might not be on the cards after all.

Brown took ages to look up, then finally:

'There have been some developments.'

Roberts dared to hope, said:

'There's been a break in the case?'

The Super shook his head, seemed weighed down with fatigue, said:

'The bomb in the canteen has put a different complexion on the whole case.'

Roberts got a real bad feeling: was he being replaced so soon? He said:

'Sir?'

'Yes, in light of this… escalation, it has been decided to pay the ransom.'

Roberts couldn't believe his ears, said:

'You've got to be kidding?'

Brown's head snapped round and he seemed to be coming out of his trance, said:

'Don't take a tone with me, laddie. You think I like this any better than you do? The powers that be want it to go away and, once everything calms down, then we can concentrate on catching them.'

Roberts tried to stay controlled but said:

'Sir, this is shite. It opens the way for every two-bit hustler to blackmail us. When word gets out we paid, we're seriously compromised.'

Brown focused and levelled his gaze on Roberts, said:

'You have your orders, sonny.'

Roberts pushed down the number of replies he wanted to give; it even crossed his mind to resign, which would have been noble. He'd packed in all notions of that after his wife died. The chances were the resignation would be accepted and then what would he do? Return to drinking gut-rot red wine? The Super raised the biscuit, held it over the tea and said:

'You're to be the bagman.'

A sad smile leaked from Roberts' mouth, the Super caught it, asked:

'What's the joke, lad?'

'Bagman, sir, that's exactly the term the bomber used.'

'So?'

'So it's ironic that we are reduced to being messengers for these kind of thugs.'

'Irony is not the business of the police.'

'Maybe it should be, is that all… sir?'

The biscuit was now immersed in the cup and Roberts had to move fast. Brown waved him away. Even outside the door, Roberts could hear the slurping begin. He wasn't looking forward to informing the team that they were fucked. Plus, he had the money to arrange. Brant was leaning against the door of his office and asked:

'How did it go?'

'Worse than you can imagine.'

Brant lit a cig, watched Roberts' face for a moment, then said:

'They're going to pay?'

Roberts thought he was all done with being surprised at Brant, asked:

'How the hell did you know that?

'No big deal, they're cowardly fucks.'

Roberts thought that Brant was taking it pretty well, said:

'You're taking it pretty well.'

Brant shrugged, went:

'Just means we'll have added motivation to get the fucks.'

Roberts wasn't sure if he meant the bombers or the brass and with Brant you never could tell. Roberts said he'd better go get the money arranged and Brant said:

'It's a fine whack of cash. You think you could slide a few hundred aside, we could have a bit of a drink with it?'

'Are you serious?'

Brant's smile was in place and he said:

'Who's going to notice a wedge off the top?'

Roberts shook his head but he did actually think about it.

Later in the day, a guy arrived from headquarters, dressed in a pinstripe suit and carrying a large briefcase. Roberts asked:

'Are you a cop or a banker?'

The man had yellow teeth, which spoiled the suit and clashed with his shining white shirt. He said:

'Is that really relevant?

'It is to me.'

'I'll need another witness while I count the money.'

Roberts couldn't believe his ears, asked:

'You didn't count it already?'

The man regarded him coldly and Roberts summoned Brant, who gave the guy a slap on the back, said:

'You're doing God's own work there, you know that?'

The guy stared at Brant as if he was something he'd found on his shoe and asked:

'And you are who, exactly?'

Brant was delighted with him, answered:

'Trouble.'

He began to extract the piles of money and put a small calculator beside them. Then in a monotonous drone he began to count. Brant waited till the guy was halfway then touched his arm, asked:

'Get you something?'

The guy was spluttering with rage, said:

'You made me lose my place, I'll have to start over.'

Roberts said nothing. The guy began again, this time, trying to keep an eye on Brant. Finally it was over and he handed a chit for Roberts to sign. When this was done, Brant asked:

'You want to go get a beer or something?'

The guy looked like he wanted to scream but in a patient voice he said:

'I don't think so.'

Brant turned to go, said:

'Fine, but I thought if you'd a few drinks you wouldn't take it so hard.'

'What are you talking about?'

Brant indicated a pile of money that was still on the table, said:

'You missed that lot or does it matter?'

It mattered.

I was for the first and probably last time in my life propositioned by a man.

'Come and have a drink,' he said.

'Where do you suggest?' I asked.

'There's a YMCA round the corner, and afterwards we could go to my place.'

I began walking away fast. He ran after me.

'What's the matter?' he said. 'Aren't you interested in queerness?'

Edward Behr, *Anyone Here Been Raped and Speaks English?*

11

ANGIE WAS IN the other room planning her great caper and Ray Cross was watching the Australian prison drama, *Oz*. He really enjoyed the brutality of the series. He'd done four years for a building society heist and his brother Jimmy had done two. He never intended returning to prison and he watched every jail drama to reinforce his conviction. He even watched *Bad Girls* and, of course, there was always the hope of a little lezzie action in that. The one sure thing you could say about Ray was he always had a drink on the go. This occasion it was Schnapps; Jimmy had boosted a Safeway and piled a lorry with every type of booze under the supermarket sun. The German spirit was going down easy and he had a nice buzz building. He stood up, stretched. Tall, he'd been told many times of his resemblance to the actor James Woods, and it made him feel good. JW was your stone psycho. Ray had *Salvador* on vid. But his all-time favourite was *The Onion Field*, where Woods played the cop-killer who, in the nick, manipulated all around him. It was the sense of total danger that Woods emanated. Ray worked on his mannerisms and pretended to be surprised when people remarked on them.

He was wearing a T-shirt with the logo:

Pog Mo Thoin

It had been given to him by a crazy Irish girl he'd been seeing. He had to let her go when she set fire to their gaff for the second time. It meant giving her a few slaps but his heart hadn't been in it. Ray felt that as Jimmy Woods had been through the mill with Sean Young, he too had to earn his spurs with crazies. In south-east London, they were easy to find. It was months later that he discovered the logo meant 'kiss my ass'. And he'd worn it ever since. Angie had tried to smarten him up, bought a stack of Ralph Lauren shirts, which he put in the Oxfam bin. The one time he'd worn them, Jimmy had said:

'You look like a pooftah.'

Gave Jimmy a hard slap to the side of the head. He'd been looking out for his brother all his life. Jimmy was a bit slow; he didn't seem to be on the same wavelength as the rest of the world and responded with a simplicity to most things. Then, in prison, he became obsessed with weights and bodybuilding and with the increased muscles he developed a sly confidence. It came from knowing that people were afraid of him. Ray was the first to exploit this new development and used him as an enforcer. Jimmy was impervious to pain and, short of shooting the fucker, he wouldn't go down. After Ray's release they'd gotten the Mews place and begun a spree of petty larceny and mild intimidation. They hadn't any huge ambition and, so long as they had beer money and some dope, they were reasonably content with their lot.

All that had changed the night they went to the strip club. Ray was hoping to exert some pressure on the manager when Angie came on the stage. The brothers watched open-mouthed. She was the most beautiful thing they'd ever seen. It would probably have never moved from their distant admiration if a punter hadn't begun hassling Angie. A bald, middle-aged git with an attitude, he was pinching her bottom and she wasn't liking it. Jimmy had moved, grabbed the guy by the collar and smashed his head on the bar, twice. Angie was impressed and when Ray asked her if she'd like to have a drink after, she agreed. They'd ended up at their place and she gave Jimmy a hand job. Then Ray got to bed her and she'd never moved on.

Slowly, she'd begun to organise their activities and the money began to roll in. Then Jimmy had found the dynamite and the whole operation moved up a notch. Ray thought it was crazy but Angie had a way of persuading them.

He said:

'It's fucked is what it is… you wanna know why?'

She gave him the sensual smile that usually signalled she was about to throw a tantrum but he carried on, said:

'See, it's the ransom money, or the extortion or whatever; you can ask what you like but the fuck is trying to collect it. The nick is full of guys who got paid then got nicked. You hear what I'm saying?'

Her tantrum had passed and she smiled, said:

'I've been working on it, that's why Jimmy has to go to work.'

He shook his head, said:

'Jimmy doesn't work, okay.'

She outlined the plan and Ray said:

'Jimmy works.'

Jimmy didn't seem to mind and once they'd got him in place he actually liked the job, began to bring home stories about the guys at work. Ray suffered this nonsense for a few days then walloped Jimmy on the back of the head, said:

'Enough with this citizen shit. You're not some kind of moron who does nine to five, you're a career criminal and once the deal goes down, you're out of there.'

Jimmy seemed hurt and asked if he could keep the uniform. Ray sighed, said, 'Yeah, yeah, keep the fucking thing,' like he gave a rats about that. Wanted to say if we pull this off, you can get a goddamn uniform made.

Angie was into it and began to stroke Jimmy, asking,

'So, the other guys, they like you, yeah?'

Ray stormed out. Angie might be sex on wheels and smart as a whip but she could be a royal pain in the butt sometimes. He walked along the Balham High Road and stopped in a pub he hadn't ever been in. Ordered a pint and took a seat. He was smoking Dunhill Luxury Length, the fancy red box you didn't see much of any more. He and Jimmy had hit a van a few weeks back and had been smoking it large ever since. It had been a long time since he'd had to resort to roll-ups; those days seemed to be long gone. He kind of missed the stuff that went with rolling your own but felt he couldn't really go back. Plus, Angie hated them and said they smacked of prison. Much as he liked Angie – she was the best woman he'd ever had – she was crazy; there was a wildness that got to be tiring. She burned brighter than anyone he'd ever known but he figured she was going to burn out fast and bring down all around her. Ray didn't intend being part of that. Once they got the dosh, he'd have to seriously consider deep-sixing her, making sure she'd never return. It was a shame but the mad bitch would have to go.

As he sank half his pint, his eyes focused on a painting on the wall. Ray knew nothing about art but this transfixed him. It was a vixen, caught as if about to take flight. She had a look of:

Danger

Sleekness

Intelligence

Sensuality.

Ray went up to the bar, asked the guy about it.

The guy was a thick fuck, said:

'I don't know shit, it's been hanging there for years.'

Ray considered, then said:

'I'll give you twenty for it.'

The guy was instantly suspicious, but pound signs were flashing in his eyes. He asked:

'How do I know the price? It might be pretty valuable, lots of people want to buy it.'

Ray finished his drink, ordered another, said:

'Have something yourself.'

The fuck took a whiskey and kept the change. As he raised his glass, he said:

'I might be tempted to let it go for £100.'

As the Americans say, Ray did the math. He'd be out the ton but he could return, in the early hours of the morning, knock the kip over, get compensated. True, he'd have to go alone as Jimmy was now a working stiff. The barman was staring intently, said:

'I know you, I mean you look like that actor, shit, what's his name?'

Ray decided to help him out, hinted

'*Salvador* ring any bells?'

'Yeah, I got it – James Belushi.'

Ray hated Belushi, took out his wallet, laid the hundred down. The guy finished his drink, said:

'Don't know about you but I could go another.'

Ray ignored him, went over, took the painting down and left without a backward glance.

Next morning, he gathered Angie and Jimmy. said:

'I want to show you something.'

Led them to the bedroom, went:

'Whatcha fink?'

Angie hated it when he spoke *common*. Jimmy asked:

'Is it a ferret? Why did you hang a ferret up?'

Angie gave a small smile, said:

'It's a vixen.'

Ray could tell by her face that she was pleased. She gave him the full look, asked:

'What's the story, Ray?'

He was hoping she'd ask, had been working on his answer all night and now, oh so casual, as if he'd just thought of it, went:

''Cos you're a fox.'

Angie kept a separate bedroom, said she couldn't bear to actually *sleep* with a person. She'd service Ray and, no matter how he coaxed, she'd leave right after. That night she gave him a sensational blow job and, as he dozed off, she went to her own room. Climbing between the sheets – it was her favourite part of the day – she could be truly alone and dream of Florida and endless days of sun and clothes.

Mostly, she found people a drag; they whined on about money and about the weather and worse, politics. All such trivial shit. What she liked was to see how they reacted to pain. Ray was okay and she didn't mind the sex. It amazed her that men would do just about anything for it. Jimmy meant as much to her as a dog she might pass in the street.

After she blew them off – and blow them she fully intended to do – she wouldn't give them another thought. First, Jimmy would be sacrificed, then Ray. She might do something special for him, take him out in a painless way. He'd bought her that dumb painting and seemed to think

60

that mangy fox was her. She played him along, kept him sweet as he was especially good on the phone. Had those cops doing somersaults. Under her pillow she kept a Browning automatic, primed and ready to lock and load. Before sleep took her, she wondered if she'd use a head or body shot on Ray. It interested her to see how the head would look if she put two into it at close range. Fuck him first then whip out the gun, say:

'Now you've come and hey, here you're gone.'

She fell asleep with a smile on her face.

Jimmy was watching the best-ever episode of *The Office*. He didn't fully understand it but now he was a working guy, he felt a kinship with it. He laughed out loud without fully understanding the humour but in the morning, when the guys mentioned bits, he'd be able to laugh all over again. Jimmy wasn't happy that it was only a temporary position, but maybe after, when they'd got the money, Ray might allow him to do a few days a week.

He'd really stayed up to watch a lezzie drama that was getting lots of publicity. Called *Tipping the Velvet*, it starred Diana Rigg's daughter. This would have impressed him more if he knew who Diana Rigg was. A big deal was being made of the fact that BBC 2 was showing it.

Ray said:

'It's porn. Just because that BBC crowd made it, doesn't change the fact that they're peddling porn. Oh, be sure to tape it, yeah?'

Jimmy was disappointed. It was tame and he had to

wade through loads of waffle for what action there was. He opened a bottle of Tequila and drank from the neck. It hit him like thunder, he was pissed before he knew it and decided to rewind the tape – maybe the show needed booze. The women looked better already.

12

FALLS AND ANDREWS were investigating a pub break-in on the Balham High Road. The owner was a thick fuck who shouted at them the second they walked in through the door:

'Who's going to pay for the damage?'

Andrews looked to Falls who asked:

'What is the extent of the damage?'

He stared at her, as if he couldn't believe his ears? Answered:

'A smashed window, broken bottles, and my dog.'

Andrews went:

'Dog?'

Now he turned to her, sneered:

'What are you, an echo? How long have you been on the job, two days?'

Falls tried not to smile, two days was exactly right. He wasn't finished:

'Yeah, my dog, they smashed his head in with something, probably a baseball bat.'

Andrews tried for a professional tone, enquired:

'What type of dog?'

'What type of dog? A fucking dead dog.'

Falls held up a finger, cautioned,

'Mind your language, sir. Now, how do you know they used baseball bats?'

He gave a vicious smile, seemed delighted she'd asked as if he'd been storing it up, said:

'Yer darkies, they use bats, they can't afford golf clubs.'

Falls wasn't put out, she was used to this crap, said:

'I see a space on the wall there. Was there a picture taken?'

The memory of the sale pleased him and he said:

'Some space cadet, he was in, having a pint and he spots the painting, has to have it. I paid, like, two nicker for it at a garage sale. Have a guess how much I got the dumb bastard for?'

As Falls didn't venture, Andrews said:

'From your tone, obviously a lot.'

'You betcha, sweetmeat: a hundred smackers, what do you think of that?'

Falls asked:

'And he was black, was he?'

The guy was confused, asked:

'Black, why?'

'Well, you said he was dumb, so I presumed he was black, given your views.'

He stared more closely at Falls, then:

'Are you fucking with me? You better remember who's paying your bloody salary.'

Andrews piped up:

'You have already been cautioned about your language.'

He gave a snort of derision, pushed past them, said:

'Bollocks.'

Andrews caught his arm, turned him and kneed him in the balls. He fell to his knees, roaring like a bull. It was hard to guess who was more surprised, him or Falls. Andrews said:

'Now you're cautioned.'

Outside, Falls said:

'I don't think they mention that in the training manual?'

Andrews smiled, said:

'Was I being over-zealous?'

'Girl, you were magnificent.'

Andrews was pleased with the praise. When Falls suggested they have a coffee, she felt she was on her way to being accepted. They went to a small café, got some locals staring at them till Falls stared back. A waitress came over, asked:

'Ladies, what can I get you?'

Falls said:

'Two large coffees and the stickiest, most calorie-laden buns you have.'

'Would you like cream on the coffee?'

Falls looked at Andrews who grinned from ear to ear. Falls said:

'Bring it on, pile on that sucker.'

Falls rooted in her bag, took out a pack of cigs, offered one.

Andrews was tempted, said:

'I quit a while ago.'

Falls lit up, said:

'Trust me, you'll be smoking again. This is the kind of job nicotine was designed for.'

The coffee came, laden with cream, and the buns were almost obscene in their richness. Falls took a spoon, scooped a dollop of cream and put it in her mouth. She made a face of simulated orgasm, went:

'Oh… oh… that's the spot… oh yes… oh my God, the earth is moving.'

Andrews got the giggles and then shovelled a spoon herself. A man in a suit was taking a dim view and glared at them. Andrews signalled him to Falls who ignored him. Then they got stuck into the buns and were like two kids, their faces a riot of cream and sticky bun. The man had had enough, marched over, said:

'This is scandalous! I mean, you're supposed to be representing the status quo. I want your names and numbers.'

He actually took out a slim red notebook and a flash gold pen, prepared to take the details. Falls drank some coffee, wiped her mouth delicately with a tissue then fixed her gaze on him, asked:

'Is that your car outside?'

'What? Oh yes, it is.'

'In about two minutes I'm going to have it towed; it matches the description of a car wanted in connection with a string of robberies. You should have it back in... oh, let's say three weeks. I obviously can't guarantee its condition but I'll ask them to be careful, you being a law-abiding citizen and all.'

He stared at her, rage creasing his brow. Then he put the notebook away and he turned on his heel, walked out. Andrews asked:

'Which car is his?'

'I've no idea.'

Andrews felt she'd learned a valuable lesson in dealing with the public.

When they went to the counter, the owner said:

'No charge, ladies, I'm honoured by your custom.'

Falls wasn't pleased, near shouted:

'Did we ask you for anything free?'

'No, but... '

'But you presumed we'd be bought for a lousy stale bun.'

She threw a pile of change on the counter and headed out. Andrews felt sorry for him, tried to give him a warm smile, it didn't seem to do much good. Outside, Falls was waiting and Andrews said:

'Wasn't that a bit harsh?'

'If you're going to have a freebie, at least make it worth-while; for a spoon of cream, you could lose your job. And, that guy would be on the phone every opportunity, asking for his favourite officers.'

'Maybe he just meant well.'

'He's the public – they never mean well.'

'I had intended him to kill somebody... spend the rest of the story making him human... I was twenty or thirty pages in before I realised he was black. Not only black, he's a black man who had tried, albeit inchoately, to turn himself into a white man, to live up to white values, at various times in his life. and they always collapse on him.'

James Sallis, on the creation of Lew Griffin.

13

ROBERTS HAD THE team gathered in the conference room. The phone was in the centre of the desk, the deadline fast approaching. Roberts had arranged for the call to be put on the speaker so they all could hear. He had the briefcase of cash beside it.

Brant said:

'So we're really going to pay these assholes?'

Roberts nodded miserably.

Porter asked:

'Have we at least a trace set on the money?'

'We are going to try and see if we can catch them when they collect.'

The team digested this, doubt writ large on their faces. Porter said:

'They seem very confident that they are going to get the money without any problem.'

Roberts' face was set in stone, as if it had been achieved over his dead body. No one seemed reassured by this. The phone rang and some of the younger officers actually jumped. Brant smiled, he was looking forward to this. The robotic voice began:

'Greetings friends, I assume I'm on speaker so I'll take the liberty of addressing you en group.'

Roberts tried to stay cool, said:

'The money is here.'

'Good man, you're a splendid errand boy. Now here's the arrangement. Are you ready because I'll only say it once, so pencils ready guys?'

Nobody moved, it was of course being taped. The voice began:

'Get a large black holdall with the word "Swag" written on it. Then Roberts you, yes you – pay attention and stop sulking – you are to deliver it to the left luggage at Waterloo station before 8.00 this evening. Get a receipt in case it goes missing, Network Rail are a whore if you don't have the ticket. That's it guys, nice and simple, so I don't see how you can fuck it up.'

Click.

Roberts looked round at the faces and said:

'Get me a black holdall and write "Swag" on it.'

Two of the officers left the room.

Roberts asked:

'Any thoughts?'

Brant leaned forward, said:

'He sounded pretty confident.'

Roberts nodded and then Porter Nash said:

'So, we deliver the money, stake out the place and then follow the pick-up – what's wrong with that picture?'

Brant said:

'It's too fucking simple. I hate it when it's too easy.'

They outlined various strategies and all had the feeling it was a waste of time. They thrashed out the numerous things that could go wrong and finally Roberts assigned the team to their roles. He then turned to Brant, asked:

'What's your gut feeling?'

'That we're going to lose the money and the gang.'

The officers returned with the bag, the word 'Swag' in huge white letters on the side.

Roberts went over the arrangements again and said:

'I'd better go.'

Brant said:

'I'll drive you.'

As they left the station, the rank and file were in the corridor to watch them go, the sight of the bag causing huge merriment until Roberts shouted:

'Get back to work.'

Traffic was heavy and Brant made some reckless moves to make time. After he'd cut up a taxi, Roberts pleaded:

'Jeez, take it easy.'

'No sweat, guv, I know what I'm doing.'

Roberts glanced at him, thought he looked positively demonic. To distract himself, he asked:

'Is everything in place?'

Brant began to light a cig, taking both hands off the wheel to do so, then actually shrugged, said:

'We have people watching the front and back, we're setting up a camera, pulling records on the staff, and you know what? It's all pissing in the wind.'

When they got to Waterloo, Brant pulled up in the no-parking zone just as his phone went.

He answered, said:

'Uh, oh, mmmph, gotcha.'

And clicked off.

Roberts said:

'You're not giving much away?'

Brant smiled, said:

'It's a party and you and me, we're going.'

'When?'

'After we dump the swag.'

Roberts thought that Brant truly was mad – not just wild, out and out barking. He shook his head but Brant went:

'Listen to me, you're not going to hang round the station. They need you, they've got your number. What you need is some R and R. When was the last time you got laid?'

'What kind of party is it?'

'The kind where you get laid.'

Then he was off, leaving the car in the no-parking zone. Roberts struggled to catch up, asked:

'You're not just leaving the car? They'll tow it.'

'Who cares, it's a piece of shit.'

'But what about the party? How will we get there?'

Brant looked back, delight on his face, said:

'See, you do want to get laid. We'll grab a cab, arrive in style; best if we don't have transport in case we get shit-faced.'

The station was crowded and the left luggage place was right at the rear, attended by a middle-aged guy in uniform. Roberts hefted the bag on to the counter and, without looking up, the guy asked:

'How long?'

When Roberts didn't answer the guy finally raised his eyes and said:

'You deaf?'

Roberts produced his warrant card, said:

'No, I'm the heat, now give me a ticket.'

Slowly, the guy began to punch out the ticket and without handing it over, said:

'Five pounds.'

Roberts snapped the ticket and said:

'You don't want to get in the way of a police operation.'

The guy was not impressed, said:

'That's corruption, that is.'

He took the bag and handed it back to Jimmy who was out the back, out of Roberts' line of vision. Jimmy immediately began to fill his overcoat with wads of money. Angie had sewn pockets all down the sides and, thanks to Her Majesty's Prison Service, her sewing was terrific. He also carried a nondescript shopping bag, which he jammed with more wedges of cash. Finally, he produced a Network Rail shoulder bag and rammed the last few packets into it. He was ready to roll. Waited until the cops had pushed off, then shouted:

'Bob, I'm gonna go get us some coffees.'

And went out the back entrance.

He was just disappearing down the steps at the side of the station when he noticed a couple of cops watching the front of the left luggage. Angie had said they'd be there and that there'd be plenty of them.

Ray was waiting in a taxi and Jimmy tore off the coat, put it and the bags on the seat, said:

'See you later.'

And he returned to work.

When he got back, Bob asked:

'Where's the coffee?'

'They were closed.'

Bob said never no mind, they'd brew their own. This included adding a drop of creature comfort in the form of Highland Grouse. It improved the hell out of whatever you were drinking. The hot drinks went down so well they batched up another lot and omitted the coffee – you can have too much of a good thing. It was Friday evening and close to knocking-off time. Soon they'd wander down to the Railworkers' Club and sink a few bitters. All in all, it was a pretty mellow way to launch the weekend. Bob was feeling very relaxed, said:

'Jim, did you hear the fashion that bloody copper spoke to me?'

'No, Bob, I missed that.'

'Yeah, the fucker, he tried to run riot, shouting the odds about being in the Met and wouldn't pay for the ticket.'

Jimmy didn't care either way and said:

'But you were able for him, I'd say.'

'Too bloody right, I don't take shit from no one. What's the big deal with the bag, do you think?'

They looked at the bag, 'Swag' in white letters almost glowing. Jimmy shrugged his shoulders and Bob asked:

'Swag! What's that about? Some kind of joke, do you think?'

'Gee, I don't know, Bob.'

The Highland Grouse was singing in old Bob and he stood, circled the bag, then bent down, said:

'Let's have a little peek; I mean, the bastards didn't even pay so it's not like they're entitled to our full protection.'

He pulled the zipper back and stared in dismay then said:

'It's empty, I could have sworn it weighed a ton, did it seem heavy to you?'

Jimmy's heart skipped a beat and he tried:

'No, it was light as a feather.'

Bob eyed the bottle of Grouse, laughed, said:

'I better ease up, eh?'

Jimmy felt relief flow over him, said:

'Let's have one for the road. What do you think, you being the senior man?'

Bob liked that tone a lot and felt they could certainly risk one more. As they closed up, the watching cops noted the time and that they weren't carrying anything.

One said:

'The only thing those guys are carrying is a feed of drink.'

A month before, Angie had rented Jimmy a small apartment in Kennington. She'd said:

'They'll check the employees and we can't be living together. I'll stay with a girlfriend so they can't connect us up.'

Jimmy was very unhappy about being on his own but she persuaded him it was only for a short time. Once the heat died down, they'd split the money and all get back together. When Ray arrived at the Mews, he had already split the money and when he handed the cash to Angie, she said:

'This seems light.'

'Yeah, I've taken half and put it someplace safe.'

She was surprised at his balls, asked:

'Don't you trust me?'

'Sure, but if anything happened to you, at least only half would be gone. This way, we need each other.'

She considered getting him into bed, see if he would reveal the location. Instinct told her it wouldn't work. He was sharper than she'd figured.

She smiled, said:

'Good thinking. When they check out the staff at the left luggage, it's possible they'll come talk to you as Jimmy's brother.'

Ray cracked a Special Brew, took a deep slug, said:

'The Mews is clean, I've sold off the hot gear. They can search all they like. Fancy a drink, to celebrate?'

'Maybe later, I have to go see about my flat.'

Ray gave her a long look, said:

'You be real careful, that's a lot of cash you're carrying.'

Angie went to a small lock-up she'd rented when she'd last got out of prison. Just off Clapham Common, it held every item that was of any value to her. Some porcelain dolls she'd nicked from an old woman, designer clothes and imitation Louis Vuiton luggage she'd found in a boot sale. The tags on the handles said, 'Florida', for the day she made her great escape and she figured it was only a short time away now. There was a portable television, a fridge, a foldaway bed and essentials like vodka, a kettle, coffee and half a gram of coke.

She laid the money on the floor and wondered why it didn't make her feel good. There and then she vowed not to go anywhere until she had it all, every last penny. It was her scheme, her planning, her fucking entitlement.

Rage enveloped her and she wanted to go back, shoot Ray in the balls, the bastard, remembering the half smile he'd given her when she'd asked:

'Don't you trust me?'

Yeah, right.

She laid out a couple of lines of coke, used a twenty from the pile to snort, and waited for the hit.

It came fast, hit her brain running and then the ice-drip down her neck. She didn't use very often as her insanity was sufficient to keep her stoked but, now and then, she'd have a hit and summon up the crystal-clear thinking she needed. As her body began to experience waves of well-being, she thought: Okay, Ray, you want to play, we'll play.

There were few things she liked better than to play, said aloud:

'Game on.'

She lifted a few loose boards from under the threadbare carpet and stashed the money. Then dabbed some perfume behind her ears. It was the brand Jimmy loved. He never tired of asking her what it was and she'd always reply the same:

'Money.'

Angie had absolutely no feelings about Jimmy, he was simply the means to an end. Sometimes he amused her but not in any fashion that she'd miss.

She took a shower, the coke singing in her veins. She was looking forward to the remainder of the evening. Naked, she assessed herself: looking good, maybe she'd cut down on the booze a bit but otherwise, in fine shape.

She selected an outfit that Jimmy usually drooled over. Stockings and suspender-belt, sheer black top and black miniskirt, add a black bomber jacket that Ray had boosted from some Europeans who'd had a place on the Balham High Road. Finally, a few lines of coke to get Jimmy off his game completely.

Leaving the place, she double-locked it and put on the deadbolt. At the end of the street was a mini-cab office and she asked for a car.

The driver, a Rasta, gave a low whistle of appreciation as she got in.

'Yo sho looking fine, girl.'

'Whatever, I need to go to Kennington.'

He had a spliff going, asked:

'You wanna get some dis good vibe?'

'I don't do drugs.'

'Yo baby, dis be life, not no drug.'

He got the car in gear and turned up the sounds. The Wailers doing their thing, he kept up a constant monologue of which Angie heard little. The music drowned him out but it didn't put as much as a dent in his rap.

When they got to Kennington, she asked the fare and he stroked his dreads, said:

'Yo like to mebbe party with me, I's got me a crib dat be shaking.'

She threw a tenner at him and a look that cut through his high, said:

'Keep the change.'

He watched her saunter down the road, said:

'No woman, no cry.'

Angie let herself into the flat.

Jimmy wasn't back yet. The place was bare, the few items Jimmy had brought were in boxes. She unpacked them, scattered them around – it had to look like he'd lived here. She piled cups and dishes in the sink. Then went to the bathroom, ran a hot bath, returned to the main room, picked up the one-bar electric fire and plugged it in near the bath. You'd get more heat from a cigarette but Angie wasn't interested in getting warm.

Then she sat down to wait. Prison had taught her how to do that, just sit and let her mind roam free. Mostly, she thought about the second half of the money – her money – and how she was going to separate Ray from it. A key turned in the lock, then she heard some fumbling and she smiled as she knew Jimmy was drunk, as he always was come evening. The door opened and he staggered in, seemed stunned to find all the lights on, then saw her and beamed:

'Angie!'

She gave a huge smile went over and put her arms round him, said:

'You tease, making a girl wait.'

He moved away from her, confusion and a hint of suspicion on his face, asked:

'Why are you here, I thought you'd be with Ray, and didn't you say we had to stay away from each other till the heat died down?'

Irritation rose in her, like he was going to get bright now, of all the times for him to start acting like a normal person. She bit down on the emotion, went to her bag, produced a bottle of champagne, said:

'But we have to have a small celebration. You did brilliant; we couldn't have pulled this off without you. I just had to come and let you know that. I even dressed special for you. Don't you like the way I look, Jimmy? Do you really want me to go?'

He didn't and she smiled to herself. There wasn't a man alive who'd turn down sex, no matter how his instinct warned him.

She purred:

'We're going to have us a killer of an evening.'

'He wore round steel-rimmed glasses that might have made someone else look like John Lennon. Marshall didn't look anything like Lennon; he looked like something that might have eaten Lennon.'
John Sanford, *Chosen Prey*

14

PORTER NASH HAD decided he needed a change of image, had been working on it for a time. Got his hair cut short and had them add a few lines of grey, just a few discreet streaks. Worked well and, even better, nobody had ragged him. When you're a cop, you daren't make major changes without them thinking you're on the take. You start to change your appearance and, to the cop mind, it says you're hiding something.

The glasses though, now they'd been a mistake. He didn't need them but he'd been watching a movie in which the guy had been wearing those steel-rimmed jobs, the type that made you look distinguished. Porter had got an identical pair and was well pleased, thought they gave an edge of seriousness with an overlay of hard-ass. Could you ask for more?

Then Brant, who else, had asked:

'Who are you… the Walrus?'

Porter hadn't got it until Brant had said:

'The glasses, you look like John Lennon's brother.'

Now he was on watch at Waterloo, keeping tabs on the left luggage office. One of the cops was staring at him, said:

'Them glasses, you look like the Gestapo.'

That was it, he swiped them off, put them in his pocket and the cop had said:

'Will you be able to see without them?'

Porter sighed, said:

'There's nothing to see, the office is closed. What are they going to do, break in?'

The cop shrugged. He had to spend the night anyway so he didn't give a toss either way.

Porter went to get a coffee and was outraged at the price, said to the assistant:

'That's a bit steep.'

'Yeah, this is a mainline station, what do you expect?'

Porter moved away, thinking everybody had an answer, none of them civil. He wondered where the hell Roberts was. Got out his phone, dialled the number. When it was answered, Porter could hardly hear for the background noise, asked:

'Chief Inspector?'

'Yes, is that you, Porter? Has there been some action?'

'Ahm, no sir, all's quiet. I was just checking in; er, are you at a party, sir?'

Brief flurry of talk, then Roberts bellowed:

'A party, when there's a major case in progress, are you out of your mind? Who's got time to play?'

'Sorry, sir, it just sounded busy where you are.'

''Course it's busy, this is London, a busy town.'

And he rang off.

Porter muttered:

'Drunk as a skunk.'

Porter Nash moved back to the watching position and asked the constable:

'Anything?'

'Not a button. You'd think there be more action in a train station.'

'It's Friday night, people have already gone home.'

The guy looked at Porter Nash, considered, then went for it:

'That's why they pay you the big bucks.'

Then to Porter's amazement, the guy took out his cigarettes. Porter said:

'Smoking? Tell me you're kidding.'

He put them away and resolved to tell the guys that Porter was as tight-assed as they'd suspected.

When Roberts had followed Brant into the house at the Oval, he'd been near-deafened from the volume of the music. Worse, it sounded like that hip-hop his daughter listened to. The front room was jammed and Roberts realised it was all women. He asked Brant:

'Aren't there any men?'

'I hope to fuck not.'

Someone pushed a drink into his hand and Brant, already with one, clinked glasses, said:

'Bottoms up.'

Roberts took a large swig, felt the liquid near burn his throat, said to Brant:

'Christ, what the hell is that?'

Brant had already finished his, was looking for a refill, peered into the glass, seemed to give it serious consideration, said:

'I'd guess tequila, what? You wanted the whole deal? Salt and lime?'

Roberts put the glass aside, said:

'No, a beer would have been nice.'

Brant was gone and a woman approached, said:

'Are you Brant's boss?'

Before he could reply, she laughed, said:

'Dumb question, right? As if anybody was his boss.'

Roberts couldn't keep his eyes off her. She was wearing one of those flimsy sheath dresses that barely covered anything. Large breasts were almost touching him, she had on killer heels and the whole outfit screamed SEX! She gave him a radiant smile, asked:

'You want to go in the bedroom?'

Brant reappeared, a barrel over his shoulder. He carefully put it down and said:

'Now, you've got beer. Stell, a glass for over here.'

Stell, who was wearing even less clothes than the one Roberts was leering at, brought a glass, bent down, got the barrel going and poured a half-pint with expertise. She handed it to Roberts and gave him what could only be called a come-on smile. Roberts grabbed Brant's arm, pulled him over to a corner, said:

'What the hell is going on? Some of these women look like hookers.'

Brant's eyes were already glazed and he seemed confused by the question, said:

'What do you mean?'

Roberts drained his glass, thought it was hot as hell in there, said:

'I'm telling you, a woman just came on to me, like a hooker would.'

Brant was staring at him and Roberts said:

'Did you hear me, I think there's a hooker here.'

Now Brant laughed out loud, said:

'They're all hookers, it's a hookers' party.'

Roberts, who'd been in all sorts of bizarre situations with Brant, couldn't believe it, said:

'You're fucking winding me up.'

Brant was unsure what Roberts' dilemma was, so tried:

'Didn't I say you'd get laid?'

'Yeah, but… '

'Well, come on, guv, you don't think normal women are going to give it up to a battered pair like us?'

Roberts didn't know whether to act offended or outraged. A woman came, took his glass and refilled it; he didn't object, nodded in a dazed way and Brant clapped his shoulder, said:

'That's the spirit.'

Roberts tried to get his head round the deal. He couldn't. Brant was having himself a hell of a time.

Roberts asked:

'This may seem a stupid question but why are we at a party thrown by hookers?'

Brant did seem to think it was a stupid question and took another huge drink then focused, said:

'They owe me and wanted to show their appreciation, and trust me, guv, there is no better appreciation than that of a grateful hooker.'

Roberts put down his glass, tried to look like he was the boss, said:

'I'll have to go, we have a major case going down and I'm... what? Hanging out with hookers.'

Brant forced another drink into Roberts' hand, nodded, said:

'Tell you what, we give it ten minutes and then we're history. What can happen in ten minutes, am I right?'

Reluctantly, Roberts agreed. Ten minutes was nothing and it wasn't as if he was pissed or anything, though he did feel a slight buzz. Brant signalled to one of the women and indicated Roberts. She smiled, began to move in their direction. The music had increased in volume and a neighbour banged at the door to complain, said he was going to call the police. He was not happy to learn they were already present before the door was slammed in his face.

Someone passed a spliff to Brant and he muttered that he'd have to report drugs on the premises before he inhaled enough weed to put a smile on even Edwina Currie's face.

He patted Roberts on the shoulder, said:

'Ten and counting, right boss?'

Falls was having a night in, she and Andrews having spent a day doing traffic and nothing, nothing on earth was as tedious as that. It also meant working with traffic wardens, and nobody moaned like those fuckers. Not even the public could rise to the level of whining achieved by wardens.

Andrews had screamed at one:

'Hey, we're trying to help you out here, we're not the goddamn enemy.'

Falls was beginning to like this girl and tried hard not to. You got close to a copper, you got hurt – it was set in stone. But this girl, she had true grit and a low level of tolerance, qualities that Falls loved. The warden tried for sympathy:

'You don't know what it's like to have to do this stuff.'

Andrews looked to Falls who gave her the okay, so she said:

'And guess what? We don't want to know. Get a real job, try doing meals on wheels or go on the dole, but primarily, stop bitching.'

Like that.

Days such as those, you wanted to get home, get wasted and shut out the world. Falls had already started. First she had a shower, then put on an old cotton dressing gown with a picture of Garfield on the front. He had a question mark over his head. Falls often wondered what the question was; it never once occurred to her to wonder about the answer.

A bottle of vodka was chilling in the fridge and that's what she wanted herself, to chill. She was drinking from a bottle of Bud and that couldn't seriously be considered drinking, could it? She liked the habit of drinking from the neck, it was laid-back and showed you were with the game. So, okay, she'd already had three but *hell!* She was home, and who was counting, anyway?

The empties sat on her coffee table, but on coasters. That proved she wasn't some kind of slob, not letting things go. She had a bag of weed in her bedside cabinet so she could seriously mellow out later. Her coke days were in the past, had to be.

She turned on the telly and swore: the ending credits were rolling on *EastEnders*. She channel-surfed until she hit MTV and there was Christina Aguilera strutting her stuff, with a song titled 'Dirty'. Falls had to look twice to make sure that, yes, she was wearing what seemed to be cowboy chaps or whatever the hell they called those leather things that went on over jeans. Lest you be in any doubt as to what the song was, the word 'Dirty' was emblazoned on Christina's knickers. Falls got into the beat of it and had to admit that the energy made you want to party.

No way was it the Bud doing the business. You'd need another ten before you could start to like Aguilera on any serious sort of level. Then a black guy called Redman joined Christina and he did that whole bad boy, gangsta rap gig. In truth it was a mess but got your motor churning.

Then Coldplay were up with 'Scientist': earnest white boys doing the Dire Straits/Travis rock-cred act. She liked this too and knew about this group as Gwyneth Paltrow was said to be pursuing an intense romance with the lead singer. Falls took a long look at the guy. He was unshaven, very pale and never smiled. Yeah, Gwynnie would love that gig.

The name of the group worked for Falls, she felt it had that nice ring of Brixton. If you had to describe how to survive the streets, you could do worse than say... 'Coldplay'... and if that didn't make sense, then you belonged in Hampstead.

She stretched out on the sofa, felt the day ease on down and thought it was nice to just fold in front of the TV and, like, hang. The niggling line 'Get a life' tried to intrude but she moved it on along. The bottle of vodka should be nicely chilled and she'd be making a run at it real soon.

The doorbell rang and it startled her. Since the days with her last man, Nelson, the bell put the fear in her, making her think that he'd come to read the riot act and drag her sorry ass off to rehab.

Dark days indeed.

'Course, she reasoned, she could just ignore it but no, here it was again, and whoever it was, they were leaning on the buzzer, determined to get an answer. Sighing deeply, she got up, went to answer it.

She threw the door open.

At first she didn't recognise the person. A blonde woman in a black bomber jacket, carrying two Tesco bags. She gave a huge smile, said:

'Hi, girlfriend!'

Angie, the woman who'd saved her purse.

Falls knew there was something wrong with this. Did she give out her address? As a rule, she never did. Cops only gave that to other cops and even then, to a very select few. But she'd been drinking vodka and her memory at such times was far from reliable.

Angie said:

'So, do I get to come in or do I just drop these goodies here and run?'

'Shit, sorry... course, come in.'

As she breezed past Falls, the smell of her perfume was downright seductive. Falls would have to ask her the brand.

Angie plonked the bags on the coffee table and surveyed the room, the empty bottles were like a neon sign.

She said:

'Cosy.'

Falls felt mortified. If it had been a man it would have been bad enough but you never wanted another woman to see you might be a slob. Especially not a classy woman like Angie.

Falls said:

'I just got home, never quite got round to tidying.'

Angie went to the bags and pulled out a bottle of vodka,

bags of crisps, peanuts, wine, carton of cigs and a mess of napkins, said:

'I didn't know what to get so I got everything.'

Falls was conscious of her ratty dressing gown and said:

'Just let me change.'

Angie put up her hand, said:

'No way, girl, you look comfortable and unless you have some guys stashed, let's have us a girlie night.'

She began to open the vodka, said:

'Yo, Elizabeth, get some glasses. We don't want to drink from the bottle – least not yet, am I right?'

Falls went to the kitchen, rinsed out some glasses, tried to get with the game. The Bud had made her fuzzy and she felt she'd better slow down and let Angie catch up.

Back to the living room and Angie was on the couch, the bottle opened. She was wearing a very short skirt and Falls marvelled at her shapely legs.

Angie caught the look, asked:

'You think my legs are too heavy.'

'No, you, ahm… you're in great shape.'

She patted the couch, said:

'Come on girl, join me.'

Falls thought she was probably imagining it but was there a tone of flirting in there? She sat back and Angie poured two lethal measures, opened a pack of peanuts, said:

'I'm, like, starved. Didn't get to eat today.'

She raised hers, clinked glasses and knocked it back. Falls took a small sip, resolved to take it real slow and asked:

'So, how come you're… in the neighbourhood?'

Angie, thinking of the one-bar fire, the bath and Jimmy, smiled, said:

'I had me a day, and I remembered we had us such a nice evening last time, I thought it would be fun to get together. Truth is, I was feeling electric.'

Falls realised she'd finished her drink and, when Angie poured two more, she didn't fight it. Angie went into a long story about the club she was working at and the shit she had to tolerate. Falls was laughing, having herself a time and thinking: I can handle this, what was I worried about?

Then Angie was talking about *Tipping The Velvet* and Falls tried to concentrate and asked:

'What?'

Angie nearly slipped it, almost mentioned that Jimmy had taped it but caught herself and said:

'Couple of babes going at it.'

'You mean, like women… together?'

Angie laughed, took a long look at Falls, then:

'For a policewoman, you're very… sheltered.'

Falls had no idea where this was going, so poured more vodka, said:

'I don't get to watch a whole lot of television.'

Angie seemed highly amused and licked her bottom lip, asked:

'Haven't you ever wondered what it's like, you know, with a woman?'

Then before she could answer, Angie went on:

'Got any music? I'd die if I couldn't have that.'

Falls went to the cabinet, selected some techno, figuring it was neutral and didn't convey any message. Angie was up, moving to the beat and then, before Falls knew what was happening, she'd put her hand on Falls' cheek, kissed her firmly.

Uncle Nate was an asshole, but he taught me one thing; if you want something, ain't nobody going to get it for you unless you get it yourself. And once you got it, make goddamn sure you held onto it.

Gary Phillips, *The Jook*

15

WHEN FALLS CAME to in the morning, she had the hangover from hell. Opening her eyes, she tried to recall the events of the evening.

She groaned as she got flashes of what happened after Angie had kissed her. It felt like battery acid was loose in her stomach and she sat up slowly.

Angie was already dressed in navy blue tracksuit and fixing her hair.

She looked over and asked:

'Elizabeth, you think I should change my hair or do you like it like this?'

Falls felt a spasm and thought she'd throw up, wondered how Angie could seem so... fresh?... Yeah, goddamn it... fresh. Hadn't she drunk at least as much as she had? The bitch was downright frisky.

Another retch hit and Angie moved over, went to touch Falls, saying:

'Ah, poor pet, not feeling so hot?'

Falls pushed her hand away and raced for the bathroom. Was violently ill. After she'd thrown up a few times, she was finally able to move to the sink and chuck cold water on her face. Then she risked a glance in the mirror.

Bad idea.

She was haggard, no other word for it. A shade of green seemed to be mixed in with the black. The eyes were red, no doubt about that. She looked totally fucked.

With a huge effort, Falls managed to sprinkle some drops into her eyes, which stung the shit out of her. She drank a half-litre of water and hoped it would stay down. Pulled herself up, said to herself:

'Okay, you can do this thing.'

Out to the kitchen where Angie was cooking! Smelled like a fry-up and Falls had to double over with a retch.

She said:

'Could you not do that?'

Angie curled her lip, fixed her eyes on Falls, asked:

'You want me to go?'

'Yes.'

As she gathered up her stuff, Falls got some water boiling. Angie said:

'Okay, I'm ready. You want to call me later, we can arrange something?'

She was at the door, looking back, with that small smile that wasn't related to warmth or humour but connected to some wires that were forever twisted. Falls pushed at the kettle, said:

'I don't think so.'

Her tone was cold and she wanted it to sound exactly that, the hangover making it easier. Angie opened the door, but paused and asked:

'What's bugging you most, Elizabeth? Is it that you slept with a woman or that you slept with a white woman?'

16

ANOTHER BOMB WENT off. Same deal, same cheap mechanism, different location.

This time it was the WH Smith bookshop on the concourse at Waterloo railway station. Not too far from the left luggage site. Panic and consternation as commuters ran for their lives. There were no casualties from the explosion but six people were hurt in the stampede.

Ray rang the police and was pissed when he didn't get Roberts.

Porter Nash, groggy from lack of sleep, fumbled for his new glasses and was seriously angry. He said:

'You asshole, the money was delivered. What the hell are you playing at?'

The robotic voice was level, amused, disguising the annoyance Ray was actually feeling. It said:

'Tell you the truth, I've got a taste for it.'

'What?'

'Where's Roberts? I don't like dealing with the hired help; you sound way too emotional to be negotiating. Not a fag, are you?'

Porter, aware he was being taped for the record, tried to rein in, said:

'You got paid, what can it benefit you to keep this going?'

'Sheee….it as our black brothers say, "I dun' tol' you young un' I got me a taste for this."'

Ray was relaxing, he was close to having fun and this cop was so easy to rile. He said:

'See, you got a clue right there. Am I a brother or playing at it, running the old double bluff?'

Porter, who'd been having chest pains and had resolved to stop smoking, signalled to McDonald for a cig. This took a minute and Porter clicked his fingers; McDonald wasn't keen on the gesture. The cig was found, a Rothmans – thus funding the South African connection anew – then a lighter.

Porter got his cigarette flamed, drew deep, said:

'The picture that comes across from all the clues I have is that you are a sick whacko and I promise you this, I am personally going to bring you down. So how you like that clue, bro'?'

And then Porter Nash did something that would become the stuff of police legend.

He slammed down the phone.

The rule is: never, never never never… hang up on a kid-napper, extortionist or hostage taker.

Then, to add to the myth, Porter collapsed.

An ambulance was called and he was rushed to St Thomas'. The paramedics, on hearing about chest pains, shot him through to Coronary Care, Porter feeeling like he was an extra in *ER*… the mad gallop through the corridors, the IV bottle, the oxygen mask, he'd have enjoyed it if the fucking pain wasn't so intense.

Porter Nash knew for certain he was dying. Gays like him liked Dolly Parton marginally better than Barbra Streisand, and her version of 'I Don't Know Much' was reeling in his head. He could hear 'I don't know much but I know I'm dying', which made it a torch song of mega echoes.

They got him hooked up to the monitors, took blood – the cocksuckers – and get this… began to question him.

Like this:

'When did the pains start?

Where are they concentrated?

Do you smoke?

Any history of heart disease in the family?'

That kind of shite.

He wanted to say:

'Fuck off.'

But he knew they wouldn't. They kept up the barrage of questions, carried on doing stuff to his chest. He could see little plastic plugs that were attached to him and the amount of tubes in his left arm was to be seen to be believed.

The specialist said:

'I would say the tube in your heart is gone.'

At least that's what it sounded like, or some valve had packed it in. To Porter Nash it all sounded like sayonara. He was finally given some painkillers and he swallowed them with relish. The truth is, he would have killed for a cig.

Like plenty of *light* smokers, he'd deluded himself by thinking he could kick any time he chose. They are the smokers the tobacco companies like best. What they do not like us to see are the poor ravaged faces of people like snooker ace Hurricane Higgins – gaunt, fucked and forlorn – peering out from the tabloids. The real maintenance comes with the guy who thinks he's not hooked. Smoking ULTRA LIGHTS and thinking the roof will never fall in.

It falls.

Porter didn't really think he could ask for ten minutes to nip out for a fast drag. Next up was x-ray… And the technician tut-tutted… 'This you do not want to hear.'

So Porter asked:

'What? You see something on there?'

'Not my job, mate. I just take the snaps, let the big boys deliver the damage.'

'So you do see something? Oh Jesus, tell me. I can take it.'

And he remembered Burt Reynolds in *The End* saying exactly the same thing, then, when he'd heard the worst, howling like a baby. The technician, putting the x-ray in a huge envelope, said:

'The porter will wheel you back.'

Porter Nash grabbed his wrist, said:

'The porter? I'm Porter, tell me the news. I'm a cop, did you know that and believe me, I can give you shit till Sunday if I want.'

The technician looked around, then whispered:

'Do you smoke?'

Oh God, it was true. The dreaded messenger was banging on the gates. Porter felt the air go out of whatever remained of his black lungs and the guy said:

'Reason I ask is, you can slide in the back there, grab a drag and I'll keep the door closed.'

PorterNash wanted to giggle, he felt hysteria rising. Smoking his cigarette and trying to get his mind in gear, he focused on a poem by Jack Mulveen he'd memorised one quiet afternoon. How the hell did it go? The title was 'The Coffin Maker's House'.

He could recall the first verse.

A creaking dilapidated sign of carved wood
Swung where a rusted steel swivel stood
A sway of Gothic letters whispering
'John Green, Coffin Maker, Est. 1919.'

The technician shouted:

'Yo, Officer, they want you.'

Ask not for whom the bloody bell tolls. He finished the cig and prayed it hadn't finished him. The porter wheeled him back upstairs and they got him a bed. He was reattached to all the tubes and the nurse asked:

'Like a cup of tea, love?'

She was black with huge luminous eyes and he thought of Falls, wondering if she knew of his plight. No sign of Roberts or Brant or indeed any cop.

He answered:

'I'd really appreciate that.'

She stared at him and he said:

'What?'

'You have lovely manners.'

What she thought was:

Fag.

When the painkillers kicked in, Porter couldn't believe the ease. He remembered Arnie's line in *Predator*:

You lose it here, you are in a world of hurt.

He began to feel sleepy, and when the tea arrived he was already dozing. A nurse came and said cheerfully:

'Mr Nash, we need some more blood.'

'You're kidding. I like, gave pints already, what's the deal?

'We need to keep an eye on your blood sugar.'

He didn't know what this meant but didn't ask for fear she'd tell him, so he said:

'My name is Porter Nash.'

She began to do shit to his arm and said:

'Impressive name.'

As she drew the blood, she was humming. There are few things as annoying as that, except for Muzak, and the worst bit is you start to try and identify the goddamn tune. He couldn't, said:

'I give up.'

She was finished and asked:

'You give up what, love?'

'The song, the one you're humming, what is it?'

She seemed lost for a moment then:

'Oh… it's "Feel".'

The sleep had retreated and he near barked:

'And that tells me what exactly?

She gave him a playful pat on the shoulder, said:

'It's Robbie Williams, he's gorgeous. Don't you listen to the radio?'

'I listen to classical music. Like, for example, yesterday, when I got home, I had Avro Pärt and then Górecki.'

Heard himself, realised he sounded like his father, like a complete prig. His dad was a highly successful businessman, had remarried the previous year. A memorable event to which Porter had taken Brant.

The father has asked Brant:

'How come you're hanging out with a fag?'

Or words to that effect.

Then he'd offered Brant a job. To Porter's everlasting delight Brant, in typical form, had said:

'I'd never work for an asshole like you.'

Brant had brought a hooker to the reception and told all her occupation. She'd done major trade in the afternoon: they weren't called working girls for nothing.

Porter had listed his father as next of kin on the admission sheet. And here he came, striding up the ward, looking like he couldn't believe people were actually taken to public wards. He was wearing a Burberry raincoat, open to reveal a blue blazer, grey slacks. A silk cravat was carelessly tied around his neck. This was his father's casual gear.

He glared at Porter in the bed, near roared:

'What's all this nonsense?'

'Hi, Dad.'

'Is it one of them faggot diseases? I don't want to catch anything.'

'They think it's my heart but they moved me out of Coronary Care, so that's a good sign.'

His father turned his head, searching for someone to order. Then said:

'You always were an idiot; only you would think there's some good sign in being hooked up to monitors.'

Porter Nash was trying to remember the name of the new wife, but no, it wouldn't yield. So he went with:

'How's the wife?'

Not a tactical plus. His father's face clouded and he said:

'Women! She thinks a credit card means free money. Your mother wasn't much better.'

'It's going well then?'

His father raised his arm and Porter smiled. How would it look if his father beat him in the bed? Then his father changed tactics, smiled his evil smile, said:

'Why am I talking to you about women? What would you know about them?'

Before Porter could answer, the doctor came and said he

needed time with his patient. Falls was walking along the ward and Porter said:

'Dad, there's one of my colleagues, will you get her some coffee?'

He stared at her then said:

'She's a nigger. I'll come tomorrow and have you transferred to a private clinic.'

Porter sighed, said:

'Don't bother.'

'What? You don't want the best care money can buy?'

'No, I don't want you to visit tomorrow or any other day.'

"At daylight I thumbed a ride with a gaunt gypsy trucker with shoulder-length hair and a death's head earring. It was 6.30 and his eyes were wide open, and he was listening to a metal band sing about the highway to hell.

'I know that highway pretty good,' I told him.

He grinned and handed me some crystal.'

Fred Willard, *Down on Ponce*.

17

ROBERTS CAME TO with the highway to hell pounding in his head. He'd had hangovers, he'd had bad hangovers but this was the *motherfucker*. This was the reference point, the level by which all future pain could be measured. He was in a bed, sorta. Hanging over the side, bile dribbling from his mouth, vomit congealed on the floor. And he was naked. He dragged himself to a sitting position and saw a woman… also naked, in the bed. He thought:

Oh God, did I?

He did.

She mumbled then suddenly sat up, opened her eyes, peered round then fixed her gaze on him, said (or rather, croaked):

'Well hello, big boy.'

Oh, Christ.

She fumbled for her bag, got it opened, pulled out a pack of Superkings, said:

'Where's my fecking lighter?'

Touch of an Irish lilt there. Found the lighter, fired up, dragged deep – one of those skull ones, where your cheek-bones disappear – and then the coughing began, ratching death-knell variety.

She said:

'Shit, that tastes great.'

One felt that irony was not her forte but if it had been…

Roberts looked round for his clothes and the door crashed open. Brant appeared, dressed in an immaculate suit, his face shining, spit and polish oozing out of him. To coin a cliché, he looked like a million dollars…or Euros, if you wanted to lean on the Irish connection. He surveyed the damage, said:

'Yah dirty dog, you sure went for it, me ol' segotia.'

Segotia?

It's an Irish word meaning… either mate or eejit.

The hooker coughed some more, then eyed Roberts with something resembling affection, asked:

'Hon', you married?'

Brant smiled, answered:

'My guv'nor was recently widowed. Tragically, we lost her.'

This was true in more senses than one. Mrs Roberts had been cremated and the two of them had gone on an almighty skite. Somewhere along the way the urn was stolen. Wherever she rested she was certainly, if not at peace, then in pieces. Rumour had it that a well-known drug dealer out of Brixton had her on his mantelpiece and stashed coke in the urn. Roberts ignored the hooker and turned to Brant:

'How come you look so dapper?'

'Got to, guv. We're the establishment, got to make an impression.'

Roberts should have known better than to expect coherence but he persisted:

'And what? You keep a change of clothes here?'

'Like the song goes, "wherever I lay my hat".'

Roberts found his clothes and they were fucked: traces of vomit and ash on them. He looked at Brant, asked:

'Any chance you'd have something I could wear?'

''Course.'

Brant disappeared and a few seconds later returned with a white tracksuit, its gold logo reading:

'I'm the business.'

Roberts said:

'Tell me you're kidding?'

'It's that or the ruined suit, guv.'

Roberts headed for the bathroom, got in the shower, turned it to scalding and steamed for five minutes. What it did was wake up his hangover, which had been in a semi-holding phase.

Not any more.

It was up on its hind legs and howling. He checked his reflection in the mirror, bad idea. Red eyes, white stubble and he thought:

How'd I get to be a wino?

Searching around, he found a lady-razor and hacked at the bristles… which hurt like a son of a bitch. There was a pounding on the door and he shouted:

'Jesus, give me a goddamn minute.'

You hung with Irish people, you ended up swearing like them. Brant, sounding highly amused, said:

'A minute you don't get… Porter is down.'

Roberts pulled on the lurid tracksuit and grabbed at a perfume bottle, splashed a sample of the contents on to his face. Big mistake, it burned like the fires of hell and he had to bite his lip to keep from crying out. He checked the name:

POISON

Roberts opened the door and Brant handed him a mug of steaming tea, said:

'Get that in you.'

He gulped it and the heat lit the roof of his mouth.

He asked:

'Is Porter shot?'

'No, heart attack. Seemingly there was another bomb and the guy called in. Porter lost it and gave himself the big one.'

Roberts was getting too much information and the Poison fumes were enveloping him. He tried to focus, said:

'Slow down, Brant, give it to me as it went down.'

Brant lit a cig, wrinkled his nose from the perfume or the smoke, or both, answered:

'There was a bomb, last night or this morning. I'm hazy

there – the same MO so it's our boys all right. Then they phoned and Porter got het up, you know how fags get, and wallop, his ticker took him down. He's at St Thomas' and the shit has really hit the fan as the Super's on the warpath. He wants to know where the hell we are.'

Roberts ran the events of the night in his head, then asked:

'They're still watching the left luggage place, tell me they haven't fucked that up?'

'As far as I know, guv.'

Roberts drank more of the tea. The strangest thing was happening: he was beginning to feel better. How could that be?'

He stared at Brant who had an enigmatic smile and asked:

'I feel a whole lot better, how could that be?'

Brant shrugged his shoulders and the hooker gave a knowing wink. Roberts smelled the tea – it was different, almost minty. The penny dropped and he snarled:

'You shithead, you spiked it, didn't you?'

'Yo, guv, time to wake up, join the revolution. You couldn't show up hung-over, could you?'

Roberts slung the tea across the room and the hooker said:

'Hey, the carpet.'

Roberts grabbed Brant's shoulder, always a dodgy move as Brant was not one to handle, said:

'I need help, I'll ask for it, you got that, Sergeant?'

'We better get a move on. The Super'll be at the station.'

Vixen

As they took their leave, the hooker handed Roberts a plastic bag and he looked the question at her. She raised her eyebrows, said:

'So I gave your gear a spin in the machine, just dry them and you're in biz.'

He was strangely touched and for a moment nearly put out his hand, but shaking hands with a hooker is not in God's scheme of things. He said:

'Thank you.'

She beamed; men showing gratitude was not a common event and said:

'My cellphone number is in there. You get frisky, you give me a call, ask for Shirl.'

They were at the door now and Brant said:

'That's it?'

'What?'

'You say thanks!'

Roberts, as per usual, was lost in the myriad turns of Brant's mind. Near shouted:

'What, you want me to send her flowers?'

Brant, who almost never showed his impatience with his boss, threw his hands up, said:

'You think they live on goodwill, on fucking food stamps? She needs paying.'

Roberts was flustered, fumbled for the right words, then:

'But didn't you do that? I mean, I thought you were their guest, the party was for you, as a return for some shady favour you did.'

Brant was hailing a taxi and said:

'Of all people, you know there's no such thing as a free lunch. How's it gonna be when you call her? She'll think, Oh, here's that cheapskate again.'

They got in the cab and Brant said to the driver:

'Waterloo station and before Friday.'

The driver, not long out of Bosnia, knew cops by smell and didn't argue. He also didn't turn on the meter. An ikon of the Black Madonna and worry beads hung from his mirror with a large sign thanking customers for not smoking. Brant lit up and Roberts had to know, asked:

'How much should I have given?'

'How good a time did you have?'

'I dunno.'

'You should have given large, like you obviously did last night. Double up when you see her.'

Roberts waved away the cig smoke and said with indignation, a difficult move to pull off when you're wearing a tracksuit that P-Daddy would shun:

'I won't be calling her. Jesus, are you crazy?'

Brant smiled, said:

''Course you will, you just don't know it yet.'

18

WATERLOO STATION WAS chaotic. Most of the end platforms were sealed off; the bomb damage, though minor, looked dramatic. Superintendent Brown, surrounded by cops, was giving it large.

His face turned purple as Roberts and Brant approached. Roberts' tracksuit seemed to glow against the dark police uniforms.

Brown shouted:

'What the hell are you wearing?'

Brant said:

'We had a lead, sir, and the Chief Inspector felt a disguise was called for.'

The Super glared, snapped:

'Did I ask you, Sergeant?'

Roberts, going with the flow, said:

'We thought we had them but it turned out to be a drug thing.'

Brown, not believing a word, said:

'And… the disguise? You couldn't bear to part with it… is that it?'

'No time, sir. As soon as we heard about the explosion, we rushed over.'

Brant enjoying the nonsense, asked:

'How is Porter Nash?'

It seemed to take Brown a physical act of will to dredge up who that was, then:

'How the bloody hell would I know? Nobody tells me anything.'

PC McDonald, on the outs for a long time, tried to gain some brownies, said:

'WPC Falls is with him.'

The Super rounded on him.

'That's supposed to be some sort of reassurance, is it? A nigger visiting a pooftah. Christ, the Force is gone down the shitter.'

The Tabloid's chief crime guy was called Dunphy. He'd recently shone in a serial cop-killing saga. He was home sick with a strep throat. His sidekick, named Malone, was filling in. When Roberts and Brant had arrived, he'd switched on his DAT-recorder. He knew those guys were always gold, he couldn't believe his luck. Moving back slowly, he slipped away, got out his cellphone. Thought: *Dunphy, you prick, you are history*. This story would make his career, he could already envisage the headline:

TOP COP CALLS UNDERLINGS
NIGGER AND POOFTAH.

Un-fucking-believable.

Roberts strode over to the left luggage office. The Super asked:

'Where are you going?'

'Checking on the ransom.'

The assembled cops looked at each other. Brown allowed himself a low chuckle, asked:

'You think we didn't already consider that. McDonald says the bag is still there.'

Brant creased his eyes, asked:

'Did he open it?'

A groan spread through the cops and a chorus of:

'What's… ?'

Brant, enunciating each word as if he were chewing on them, asked:

'The bag… did he open it?'

A mad scramble to the luggage office.

Bill, the attendant, still suffering from Friday's hang-over and the after-effects of the bomb blast, shouted:

'Hey, take it easy.'

As Bill was trampled by cops, Brown tore open the bag. They could see it was empty. He pointed at Bill, ordered:

'Arrest him!'

Bill's arrest was a sensation. Reporters, TV crews besieged the police station. Roberts tried to reason with Brown, said:

'It's not him.'

The Super, flush with pride, relief and a mad belief that the nightmare was over, allowed himself a supercilious smile, answered:

'Oh, it's him all right. When you've been in this game as long as me, laddie, you just *know*.'

Brant, behind Roberts, was more than happy to have Brown expose himself as a horse's ass. It might even result in them getting shot of the bastard. Not even the Masonic Lodge would save him. But Brant didn't want Roberts to go down with the fuck, tried to pull him away. Roberts, his hangover resurfacing, was livid, said:

'Sir, with all due respect, this is balls. We're going to appear extremely foolish.'

Before, Brown would have slapped down his Chief Inspector for the tone of impertinence. But drunk with success, he turned to the other officers, his hands, palms outwards in the mode of *'Lord, grant me patience'*, said:

'Did you hear that, men? Our Chief Inspector believes we're going to look foolish. I ask you, man to man, can a policeman dressed in a white pimp tracksuit truly appreciate the term "foolish"?'

It got the required jeers, guffaws, derision. Though the officers liked Roberts and were afraid of Brant, they went with the Higher Authority. Brown was elated; he couldn't recall the last time he'd felt camaraderie with the troops. He said:

'Drinks on me, lads.'

Big hurrahs and cheers of 'For he's a jolly good super'.

Roberts was left with Brant.

He wanted to shout after Brown:

'You ignorant prick.'

Brant, his body relaxed, got his cigs out, fired up, said:

'Let's have a look at the other employee.'

'What?'

'The other guy in the left luggage office, I see he didn't show up for work. What do you say we pay him a visit?'

Roberts gave a large grin.

'Mignonette,' repeated the waiter, thinking visibly. Which would be worse, thought Bobby; telling Eddie Fucking Fish, known gangster associate, that he couldn't have the fucking mignonette with his oysters – or approaching a rampaging prick of a three-star chef in the middle of the rush hour and telling him to start hunting up some shallots and red wine vinegar?

Anthony Bourdain, *Bobby Gold*.

19

IT TOOK A time for Roberts and Brant to get the address for Jimmy Cross. They put his name in the computer and Brant said:

'Bingo.'

Jimmy's previous was burglary, petty theft and a little light mugging. He'd done time with his brother, Ray. Roberts made a note of where Ray lived, turned to Brant and summarised:

'Jimmy hasn't been too long in the luggage biz and only recently moved to the bedsit in Kennington. Seems he's not the brightest tool in the box.'

Brant continued to read the files, added:

'Now, Ray, he's a whole different deal. We're talking career criminal and he seems to be a wide boy. Jimmy follows the lead set by Ray.'

Roberts got some tea, handed a cup to Brant who asked:

'What, no Club Milks?'

'Don't you have a hangover?'

Brant drank the tea noisily, lit a cig, said:

'Hangover? Naw, I take precautions. Jeez, I could murder a Club Milk. What you do is get a wedge of that chocolate, pop it in your mouth, slurp in the tea, sugared of course, then add the layer of nicotine.'

Roberts wanted to know how to prevent a hangover. Who doesn't? But he was so taken with Brant's description of how to enjoy a Club Milk, he let it slide. He could only hope Brant was kidding. Yet, in their years together, he'd seen him pour scotch on curry, add milk to Baileys and once, memorably, coat chips with brown and red sauce together.

Go figure.

He shuddered, put it from his mind and asked:

'You think we should tool up?'

Brant, never usually averse to weapons, shook his head.

'Not Jimmy. Let's see him then we can decide if we need hardware for the brother.'

They went to get a vehicle from the car-pool.

When they saw it, Roberts sighed, asked:

'Why is it always a bloody Volvo?'

Brant, getting behind the wheel, answered:

'Could be worse, McDonald could be driving us.'

The said PC McDonald had been watching them, eavesdropping on their talk, heard them agree to visit Jimmy.

When they'd gone, he booted up the computer, down-loaded the file and decided he'd go after Ray.

20

THE FIRST SHOT took McDonald high in the shoulder. The second, a head shot, knocked him down. Ray Cross thought he'd killed him, hesitated, then stepped over the copper and ran for all he was worth. He couldn't believe they were on to him so fast. The past 24 hours had been among the most shocking of his erratic life: having the money, successfully planting bombs, he should have been over the moon. Instead he was on the dark side of it.

It had begun with him acting purely on instinct, playing a hunch. Jimmy was heavy on his mind and it was the first time Jimmy had been on his own. In the flat by himself, he was bound to panic. So, despite the resolution to stay apart until the storm had passed, Ray went on over.

He had a key, which Angie didn't know about. There were a lot of things he didn't tell the Vixen. As soon as he

opened the door, he knew it was bad. The smell of…
what?… like singed leather or worse. He took a deep
breath, said:

'Jimmy, yo buddy, you okay? It's Ray, where are you,
pal?'

No answer.

The sitting room was in shadow and he pulled open the
curtains, the light from the street illuminating the furniture. An empty bottle of champagne sat on the coffee table.
Möet, the expensive one – as if Jimmy knew the frigging
difference between that and cider. So, Angie had been
around, the champers was like a signature.

This was bad.

Another smell, this one … weed. Jimmy liked a smoke.
Silver paper on the floor pointed to the old nose candy: a
real party all right. He nearly smiled at how he hadn't been
invited.

Ray walked slowly towards the bathroom, shoved the
door open and gagged.

Fried fritters… that's what he thought. Of all the mad,
insane connections… What remained of Jimmy was
burned to a cinder. Ray felt his stomach heave and then the
vomit came gurgling up, like some minor *Exorcist* stunt.
Flew like a projectile across the room. Sweat poured down
his back and he felt his shirt drench in perspiration.

He heard a moaning and realised it was his own howl of
anguish. Staggering out to the front room, he searched
round, found a bottle of tequila – Jimmy always liked the
odd ones – and tore off the cap, swallowed a huge gulp.

Stay or up chuck, the ballet in his stomach raged. Then the Mexican took over and he felt the warmth begin to caress his guts. Took another large wallop and lit a cig, the trembling passing. He whispered:

'Jimmy… Jesus… Jimmy… oh, God.'

Returned to the bathroom and approached the thing in the bath. Saw the electric fire near Jimmy's feet. He could see how it went. Angie, dressed to kill – yeah, in the fuck-me heels, short skirt – making Jimmy delirious with sex. Teasing, booze, dope and into the bath, coaxing. Jimmy would have jumped out of a window for her. Then setting up the fire, cooing:

'We don't want you cold, do we, pet?'

He could see her, standing over the bath, Jimmy gasping from desire and her touching the rim of the fire, then:

SPLASH!

The ferocious crackling and twisting of the current as Jimmy was hot-wired. You ever got to ask Angie about it, she'd say:

'Well, he went clean.'

His eyes lit on the box of Radox, half empty, a real Angie touch. He muttered:

'Goodbye, buddy.'

Turned and got the hell out of there.

Went to Clapham, bought a gun. Just off the Common, a retired army guy, get you any hardware at short notice. He hadn't been wild about the late-night roust, like Ray gave a fuck, and he said:

'It's a little short notice.'

Ray had met him in the nick, didn't feel he had to explain and said:

'I need something fast, you can do that or not?'

He did the all-important thing, he showed cash, a lot of it.

The guy could do it.

But was apologetic, said:

'Thing is, like I said, short notice, all I got is some .38s, that do you?'

Ray liked the .38, it was handy; you could carry it without too much bulk and as he was familiar with it, he didn't have to worry about dry firing. Lock and load. He asked:

'Ammunition?'

Now the guy smiled, a rare sight. When a gun dealer does that, look behind you and often.

He asked:

'Does a nigger like baseball caps?'

Ray gave a tight smile, nothing to do with humour but let the fuck know he'd heard that, like, a 1000 times and it was old then. He laid out a wedge and the guy went:

'Uh huh… ?'

Translation: *more*.

Ray laid out a few extra and the guy went out and got the piece and a box of ammo, put the goods in a McDonald's bag. Seeing Ray's look, he said:

'I like to give them the business.'

Ray took the bag, said:

'They can't make coffee for shit.'

The guy was shaking his head, replied:

'It's not the coffee, it's the ambience… take a mo' in the Walworth Road branch late on a Friday night, you'll get my drift.'

Ray hadn't slept. Holding the weapon in his hand, he paced all night, remembering moments with Jimmy. A feeling of total disbelief vying with raw rage, he tried to focus on where Angie would hole up and realised he knew very little about her, save she was a cold bitch.

A stone killer and what's more, she had half the money – half Jimmy's money.

Smoking a chain of Dunhills, chugging Special Brews until he was demented. Time to time, he'd pick up the .38, aim, shout obscenities. So it was when McDonald banged on the door. Ray, in a haze, opened and seeing the uniform, the gun was up and he was firing

What the fuck happened?

He stepped over the guy, ran for all he was worth.

21

BRANT AND ROBERTS hammered on Jimmy's door and got the smell, nodded. Brant stepped back, raised his boot and gave a ferocious kick. The door came down without a whimper.

Roberts said:

'Maybe we should have tooled up.'

Brant was on high alert, answered:

'Too fucking late now.'

Went in low and fast, rolled on the floor and came up in a semi-crouch, said:

'Police.'

Roberts was stunned, walked in, asked:

'Where did you learn that shit?'

'Saw it on *NYPD Blue*.'

Roberts could tell there was no one in the flat, no one

alive anyway. The stench was a familiar one, was all over bar the tagging. Brant headed for the bathroom, entered slowly, said:

'Oh fuck, I think I found Jimmy.'

Together, they stared at the burned hunk and Brant indicated the electric fire, said:

'Gee, how careless.'

Roberts said:

'They took him out.'

'They?'

Roberts was on his cellphone, calling an ambulance, scene of crime guys, the whole outfit.

Brant said:

'I'm impressed.'

Roberts said:

'I want this place gone over with a fine comb: finger-prints, the empty bottles out there, the lot. And get a crew over to his brother's place, tell them to arm up.'

Brant was on his phone and shaking his head, went:

'Too late. You're not going to like this. Fuck, you are going to hate this.'

'What?'

Brant fumbled for his cigs and for the first time ever, Roberts noticed a tremor in his hand, knew it had to be bad. Nothing shook Brant, not since he was indirectly responsible for the death of a young cop some years back. Brant moved past him, grabbed a bottle, looked disinter-estedly at the label, tequila, shrugged and drank deep. Shuddered, said:

'That stupid prick McDonald, he must have been listening to us, he decided to check out Ray alone and he got shot.'

'Dead?'

'As good as, could be a headshot.'

They knew how that went, you were fucked either way; never came back from the head stuff, not in any way worthwhile. Brant took another slug, offered the bottle. Roberts shook his head, said:

'This is getting seriously fucked.'

In a little while the place was swarming with technicians, all of whom had watched too much *CSI: Crime Scene Investigation* and acted accordingly. Roberts gave his instructions and moved outside with Brant, said:

'Any word on Porter?'

'Shit, I forgot all about the pooftah.'

Roberts gave him the look, said:

'I thought you guys were friends.'

'Yeah, so?'

'So, how come you call him names?'

Brant, the tequila already showing in his eyes, said:

'You should hear what I call you.'

22

FALLS FINALLY GOT to talk to Porter after the doctor had taken an inordinate amount of time with him. From the corridor, she could see them and, by Porter's expression, it wasn't good.

Porter's father had completely ignored her. She wasn't too pushed: bigotry was as familiar to Falls as egg and chips.

Then the doctor moved away and she approached. She hadn't had time to bring anything and if she had, what could she have thought of to bring someone in Coronary Care? Porter looked awful, ashen... and all those tubes in his arms. She began:

'You gave us some fright there.'

He sat up in the bed, stared at her, asked:

'No grapes?'

'Sour ones maybe?'

He smiled and she felt extraordinary relief. It was a long time since he'd done that, leastways for her. Not his fault, he'd tried everything to stay friends but with his promotion and the shit in her life, she had punished him. I mean, it's what you do, you make the close ones pay for the grief you get, I mean… that's how the world works, right?

She reached for his hand and asked:

'How are you?'

'Well, I was scared but that passed. I'm a cop, scared is what we know, so now it's settled into serious anxiety.'

She knew that song, had tried to still it with buckets of coke and oceans of vodka. She squeezed his fingers and he gave a huge smile and, not for the first time, she wished he wasn't gay. Then, with a rush, she recalled her night with Angie and thought, Maybe we've more in common now.

She moved her hand, fixed his hair and asked:

'So, what's the deal?'

He sighed and she wasn't sure she wanted to hear the reply but kept her face neutral and he said:

'My heart is okay, thank God, but they were concerned about what caused the collapse. Asked a barrage of questions; worse than cops these guys and with the worst verdict in the wings, they have more juice than us. I said I'd been losing weight, had a constant dry mouth and seemed to spend my life going for a pee – it's diabetes.'

'What?'

'Yeah, bummer, right? You can have it for ages and not

know, then stress or some such will trigger it and I was going into insulin shock.'

Falls' imagination conjured up needles and having to inject yourself daily, like some desperate junkie. He said:

'It's not so bad, eh? I mean, if my heart was fucked, I'd be, like, gone.'

She had to ask, so she did:

'Are you going to have to… ahm, do the insulin gig…?'

He seemed to lose focus for a moment, then:

'There's two types and I don't know yet if I'm one or two. One is tablets, the other is shots.'

Shots. She'd only moments before heard about McDonald and hadn't even allowed herself to digest that and she didn't think it was the time to tell Porter.

She said:

'Let's root for the tablets, yeah?'

He pressed her hand and said:

'Thanks for coming.'

Seemed like a window to mention the previous months so she tried:

'I haven't been, like, you know… very nice to you. I, ahm, I was not in the best of shape.'

Lame, it sounded so goddamn lame. He tried to wave it away but she had to push for herself too.

She went on:

'I was a complete bitch. And… I'm sorry.'

He seemed embarrassed so she moved on, asked:

'Need anything? Pyjamas, deodorant?'

His smile was returning and he said:

'Yeah, a sweet guy.'

She was shaking her head:

'No such thing.'

A nurse came to fluff his pillows and he asked:

'What's with the pillows? That's the third time already.'

The nurse was unfazed, said:

'It looks like we care.'

'About the pillows?'

Falls looked at the nurse who raised her eyes to heaven and Falls said to Porter:

'I think you're on the mend.'

The nurse, with a concerned expression, asked:

'Did you know that policeman who was shot?'

Falls sighed, and Porter sat up, alarm writ huge, asked:

'What?'

Anyone could hang a man, and quite a few people could pull a lever that released cyanide into an air-tight room. A fewer number could probably electrocute a human; that was a job frequently botched. The half-burned corpse still twitching, requiring another thirty-second jolt of fourteen hundred volts, the lights dim again in the prison library… But hardly anyone outside the medical profession could be found qualified to measure a lethal dose of poison and neatly prepare a man for the injection of it.

Jim Nisbet, *Lethal Injection*.

23

ANGIE WAS FOND of poison. In the club, the girls kept a store for awkward punters. A guy got stroppy, he got a tiny amount in his drink, not enough to do serious damage but ensured he'd have stomach cramps from hell and the runs, plus maybe a jolly to the hospital. The cheap fucks, the ones that tipped like misers, they got a shot of it too. Some of the girls believed a tiny amount kept your weight down and aided the complexion; it's not for nothing they've been called poisonous. Angie had helped herself to a wedge on leaving.

Now she was holed up with a stripper named Rachel in a studio rental off the Balham High Road. Rachel was a pain in the ass, always whining, checking the fridge and going:

'Did you touch my Evian?'

And her low-fat yoghurt... God forbid you looked side-ways at that shit. Angie wasn't entirely sure but it did seem as if there was a pencil mark on the booze bottles. Rachel was a big girl, had been round the block a few times and was showing the mileage. She'd had her breasts inflated and was forever checking for droop. Angie thought she resembled Jordan's mother but reassured her she was foxy. The rental seemed to shrink as the days passed – it had been a week since the copper got shot.

Rachel, looking at Angie, had asked as Ray's photo flashed on the telly:

'Hey, didn't you hang with that guy?'

And got her first dose of arsenic.

What Rachel liked was to sit down for breakfast, the whole works. Little chintz tablecloth, a lone flower, grapefruit juice and muesli, decaffeinated coffee with low-fat milk. Angie went along with this crap as she needed the hideout.

She took her time, then:

'Ray? Not any more, I blew him out.'

Rachel was curious and persisted:

'I thought he was kinda cute. You think he really shot the policeman?'

Angie asked for a napkin and when Rachel went to fetch them, she sprinkled a little of the poison on the muesli, stirred it in.

When Rachel returned Angie said:

'No, it's a mistake, Ray wasn't the type to carry. He hated guns.'

Watched as Rachel spooned the cereal and made a face, said:

'This tastes a bit bitter.'

Angie was ready and relished the fun, always it was the game and she sure loved to play, said:

'It's the lemon juice.'

'What? We don't have lemon.'

'See my complexion, isn't it great?'

Rachel looked at her with admiration, gushed:

'Oh yes, how do you do that?'

'Lemon juice, a few drops daily and you can cut your cosmetics in half.'

Rachel dug in like her life depended on it. Angie had never seen anyone die from poisoning and was hot to see how it'd go. She'd do it nice and slow, see how it went. If Rachel got any more curious, she'd just up the ante and finish the cow off.

Sure enough, the next day, Rachel was sick as a parrot – vomiting, diarrhoea, the works. Angie was the soul of comfort, plying her with water, cold faceclothes and dancing attendance.

Rachel, groaning, said:

'It must be something I ate.'

'Kebab. You have to pack those in.'

'But you had one, no, you had two.'

'See, Rachel, I can eat anything, but you're so delicate, you have to be careful. Don't worry about a thing, I'll take care of you.'

Would she ever.

Angie had completely altered her appearance. Shorn the blonde hair, applied a jet-black colour and added horn-rimmed glasses. When Rachel saw her she shrieked:

'Oh my God.'

Sounding like Phoebe in *Friends*… which is sounding like horror.

Angie, pleased with her appearance, said:

'I've met a new guy and he's sort of conservative. I want to fit in with his job.'

Rachel's reply was cut off by another bout of throwing up.

24

IN BRIGHTON, RAY was also sporting a new image. He'd dyed his hair red, also got glasses, a pair not unlike the ones Porter Nash had so recently abandoned. He looked like Ginger Evans' brother, a nightmare of a whole other hue. He was staying in B&B near the pier... well, what used to be the pier till the storms blew it to fuck and away. Ray was grieved, he'd loved that boardwalk; reminded him of the childhood he wished he'd had.

Going down to the seaside for long summer days, riding the donkeys, buying the slightly naughty postcards with the fat lady saying rude things and sucking on an ice-cream cone. Then, candy floss and fish 'n' chips wrapped in newspaper.

The reality was a drunk for a father and a mother on the game. Once, after they'd got out of nick, Ray brought

Jimmy down here and they'd spent a weekend getting shit-faced, taunting the gays who cruised the promenade, and trying jellied ells. Jimmy had loved that holiday and they'd sworn when they'd got the big score, they'd come down and stay in The Grand.

Sitting on his bed in the boarding house, Ray toyed with the .38 and forced himself to wipe Jimmy from his mind. Jimmy was getting a cheap box in some pissy pauper's grave and Angie was, no doubt, living it large. Sure, she'd got clean away. The whole of the police force was out looking for him and there wasn't a minor villain who wouldn't sell him out.

Ray had two objectives:

One, find and kill Angie;

Two, get Jimmy's share of the cash.

He had Angie's cellphone number and hadn't yet called. She'd have kept the phone as she wanted the money too. The one sure thing about her, she worshipped cash and when she felt she was owed, she'd do whatever it took to get it.

He'd be calling her.

Brant was visiting Porter Nash.

They'd kept him in hospital until his blood levels settled. He was sitting in the corridor, sneaking a cig – hadn't yet applied the patches as he'd been instructed. Brant was dressed in a dark navy suit, police federation tie (stolen) and heavy, handmade Italian shoes. He looked like a mafioso, had a cig in the corner of his mouth and had been cautioned twice by staff. Porter was glad to see him. They'd forged the most unlikely of friendships and it was a mystery to them both. But they didn't sweat it and just figured it was beyond analysis. Brant handed over a book, said:

'Thought you'd need some reading.'

Porter sighed, he knew it would be Ed McBain – with Brant it always was. Sure enough, a fat hardback with the title *Fat Ollie's Book*.

Brant said:

'It's a cracker. Fat Ollie writes a novel and it gets stolen shit, all you'd need to know about writing is in there.'

Porter put the book aside, said:

'I appreciate it.'

Brant stubbed the cig on the floor and Porter tried not to notice, asked:

'What's the news on McDonald?'

'He's still in intensive care, head shot, you know, tricky number.'

'Will he make it?'

'I think he'll live, but will he make it? I doubt it.'

This was Brant at his cryptic best and Porter knew better than to go there. Porter was aware of the detestation Brant felt for McDonald but he'd never like to have a cop hit, no matter how big an asshole he was.

Brant asked:

'So, what's the deal with this diabetes gig? You going to be shooting up like some sort of civilian junkie?'

Porter didn't rise to the bait, said:

'I have type two, which means I'm on tablets for the foreseeable future. You want to know the hardest bit?'

Brant looked vaguely bored, said:

'If you want to tell me.'

'Salt.'

'That's it?'

Porter could have told him of all the dietary changes, the new regime of health, the constant blood checks, the fear, but Brant wasn't the type to give a whole lot of attention to this. So, he said:

'I love salt, in fact I adore it, cover everything with it and now, no more. I can't taste my food now, isn't that a bitch?'

Brant was staring at a nurse's legs and said:

'What's a bitch is we can't get a line on Ray. He's gone to ground and believe me, we've pulled out all the stops; what we have got is a chick who used to hang with the brothers, but gee, guess what? She's gone to ground too.'

Porter knew now that Ray was the guy he'd been on the phone with and he wanted this guy so bad, he could – as the Yanks say – *taste it*. He wanted Ray in his hands, up close and real personal; he tried to rein in the rage that had reared up – the doctors had emphasised that stress was perilous to his condition.

He took a deep breath and saw that Brant was smiling, asked:

'What?'

Brant peeled the wrapper off a Juicy Fruit, split it in half and offered a wedge. Porter shook his head and Brant said:

147

'You've got a hard-on for this guy, no offence to your orientation by the way, but you want this guy so bad, you need to step back, cool off, 'cos all you're going to get is fucked. You can't get them when you're het up; trust me, I've been down that road.'

Porter Nash's rage moved up a notch and he felt a twinge in his chest, he snarled:

'Gimme a cig.'

'Whoa, buddy, where did those famous manners go?'

He took out the pack of Weights, only available in the West End, and gave one over, if grudgingly. Lit him up with a battered Zippo that had the logo '1968' stamped on it.

It still made Brant smile when he recalled how he'd nicked it.

A passing porter stopped. Demanded:

'What are you people thinking of?'

He pointed his finger at the plethora of 'No Smoking' signs, and Brant said:

'What I'm thinking is... will I sink my shoe in your hole or will I let my ranking officer do the honours?'

The porter took off quick.

Porter Nash looked at Brant, asked:

'I need your word.'

'Depends, old pal.'

'When you get a line on Ray, you give me a bell.'

Brant seemed to consider, then:

'What's the barter?'

'Excuse me?'

Brant laughed, he enjoyed this, said:

'You're my mate, no question, even if you're a fag, but how I work is, I do something for you, you owe me, got it?'

Porter Nash nodded; he got it.

Big time.

25

FALLS AND ANDREWS were called to a domestic. The husband had been beating on the wife for two hours. The disturbance was at a block of flats in Meadow Road. Falls cautioned:

'Follow my lead on this, these can get nasty very fast.'

Andrews nodded but Falls was uneasy about the gung-ho expression she was wearing. She emphasised:

'I'm serious, watch the woman.'

'Isn't she the one who got beaten?'

'Yes, but if you decide to cuff hubby, they suddenly have a change of heart.'

Falls banged on the door and it was opened by a small boy; he looked petrified.

Andrews asked:

'Can we come in?'

'Dunno.'

'We'll just be a minute.'

'But Dad is beating on Mum and he doesn't like to be bothered.'

Falls moved him outside, said:

'You wait here, we'll only be a minute.'

They ventured slowly in, the sound of a woman crying in their ears. Turned into a sitting room, a scene of chaos. A TV had a hole in the screen and every stick of furniture was smashed. A woman was huddled in the corner, weeping. They heard the toilet flush and then the man appeared, zipping up his flies. He was small, about five four, dressed in a raggedy T-shirt, dirty jeans and barefoot. He was wiping his mouth and seemed unfazed by them, asked:

'What you cunts want?'

Falls walked over and turned as if to address Andrews, used her elbow to hit him in the stomach. He went down with a whimper. Andrews was about to speak when the woman launched and landed on her back, sinking her teeth into Andrews' neck. The joint screaming and howling would have put a banshee to shame.

Falls marched over and pulled her baton, lashed the woman on the skull. You get a biter, you can't fuck around; it's not the time for negotiation. Let the stick do the therapy.

The woman fell off like a downed Man-U prima donna. Andrews, in shock, was sobbing. The man on the floor began to sit up so Falls gave him a tap to the side of the head and finished his song.

She got out her radio, shouted:

'We've got an officer down, two perps in need of aid and SEND SOME FUCKING BACK-UP!'

She moved into the kitchen, spotted an open bottle of scotch, brought it out, tilted it to Andrews' neck, and poured. If Andrews had howled before, it was nothing to the cry of anguish she gave now. Falls tried not to think of Rosie, her best friend, who'd been bitten by a junkie and after Aids testing, took her own life.

The booze revived Andrews and she managed to complain:

'What were you thinking, that hurt more than the bite?'

Falls was seriously angry, pulled Andrews round, said:

'What did I tell you? What the fuck did I tell you? Not to turn your back on a woman in a disturbance... and what do you do?... You turn your friggin' back... Do you know how serious a bite can be? Do you have any bloody idea of how that can go, you stupid bitch? ...You think I can afford to lose another partner?'

And realised she was shaking Andrews so violently that the WPC was returning to shock mode. She let go and grabbed the bottle. Took a huge wallop. The guy on the floor opened an eye, asked:

'Could I maybe get a snort of that?'

26

BRANT HAD TO get a new snitch. Despite the new technology – DNA testing, computer databases, profiling, door-to-door enquiries – nothing could touch the informer for results. It was the very lifeblood of the deal. Brant had a shocking record with them. Not that they didn't pay dividends; on the contrary, they had helped break many a case but the fatalities were massive.

His last two had, respectively, been kebabed and drowned in a toilet. Word was out that if you talked to him, you ended up dead and in horrible fashion. Plus, the villains were an added peril; they heard you were talking to him, sayonara sucker.

Alcazar was a well-known character around the watering holes of south-east London. Known as Caz, he had a history of hanging paper, dealing in dodgy traveller's cheques and his latest venture – the cyber-café racket – had done very nicely for a brief time. But that had gone belly up and a stint with hot cellphones hadn't lasted.

His history was the stuff of legend. Various times, he was from Puerto Rico, South America, Honduras, Nicaragua. What made him stand out from the herd was that he'd never done time. Brushing as close to the line as he did, it was a bloody miracle he'd never been sent down. And people liked him, he had a way of ingratiating himself to everybody. He was short, with coal-black hair, pitted skin and the body of a dancer. Hooded eyes that some hooker, in a bout of absinthe, termed 'smouldering'.

The boy could dance, no argument. A woman will forgive a rogue for most things if he can do that. Flamenco, Salsa, the Margarena, he had all the moves. Jiving, that old neglected classic, he could do to perfection. You want to make a woman laugh with delight, get her to jive, and if she's delighted, bed is already made. He could swing a woman halfway round the floor, with a perilous edge of almost losing her and therein is the art, to bring it right to the precipice and hold on. A joy to behold, it was most fascinating to observe men as he did his thing. They sneered and muttered 'faggot', wishing with every fibre of their being that they could have the balls to dance like that.

The streets being the danger they were, Caz had to have some protection. A lot of irate husbands eyed him. His weapon of choice was the stiletto, much forgotten since the appearance of the Stanley knife and, of course, the obsequious baseball bat. In the heyday of the Teddy Boys – was there ever a more fun time? – you packed a flick-knife along with the Brylcream. A cold fascination in the way you hit that little button and the blade snapped out like the worst kind of lethal news.

Caz had the sex and danger to a fine craft. Got the woman to the bed, slipped out the stiletto and snapped the bra-strap with the steel, then said:

'You want me to hit another button?'

Did they ever – and often.

Caz could move with ease in almost any company, which made him an ideal snitch; it would have also helped in an Inland Revenue career. Brant found him in a Mexican place, late in the afternoon, asked:

'You know me?'

Caz tried to raise his famous smile, failed, said:

'Senor Brant, of course. You are legend, is not so, amigo?'

Brant signalled to the waitress who was dressed in fla-menco gear, with the name tag, 'Rosalita'. She sashayed over, lisped:

'Si, senor?'

She was from Peckham.

Brant looked at Caz, asked:

'What's good?'

'San Miguel and the enchilada is *muy bueno*.'

Brant sighed, ordered:

'Two of them Miguels and before Tuesday.'

Brant reached over to Caz's cigs, read the packet – Ducados – took one, fired it up, coughed, said:

'Jeez, what a piece of shit.'

He didn't stub it out, said:

'First off, I'm not your amigo, got it? You ever call me that, I'll break your nose. Second, you are now working for me and I need information. Everything on Ray Cross and the blonde chick he ran with, I need this like yesterday.'

Before Caz could reply, Brant held up his hand, said:

'This is not negotiable. I don't want to hear dick about how hazardous it might be, 'cos I'm the most dangerous item that can fall on you. Now, are we clear, amigo?'

They were.

'It's ungovernable… Psychosis is everywhere, in your armpit, under your shoe. You can smell it in the sweat in this room… we're all baby killers, repressed or not… how do you measure a man's rage? Either we behave like robots, or we kill. Why do you expect your police force to be any less crazy than you?

Jerome Charyn, *The Issac Quartet.*

27

CAZ SURPRISED EVERYONE, especially himself, by coming up with the goods so quickly. He met with Brant at the Cricketers, said:

'I got a result.'

Caz was wearing what could only be described as a garish shirt, something Elvis would have worn for *Elvis in Hawaii*. He was even wearing a large gold medallion on his exposed chest. Brant, yet again in a bespoke suit, asked:

'Where did you get the shirt?'

'Like it? I can get you one just like it, or would you prefer a more colourful shade?'

The horrendous thing was, he was serious.

Brant stared at the medallion.

Caz said:

'It's Our Lady of Guadeloupe… but I can't get you one

as my sainted mother, God rest her, gave it to me when I escaped from El Salvador.'

This was far too much data for Brant, who said:

'El Salvador? I checked on you, boyo, you were brought up in Croydon.'

Caz looked defeated – crestfallen just wouldn't do justice to how his face appeared – and he tried:

'Not too many people know that.'

Brant gave him a hard slap on the face, said:

'Get the drinks in. You behave yourself and you can be from fucking Nigeria if you like. Now hop on up there. A large Teachers for me, and some cheese and onion... go.'

Caz was attempting to focus, whined:

'But don't you want to hear my news?'

'What's the hurry?'

And Caz got the look. He moved rapidly to the bar. The barman had a pony-tail, a checked waistcoat and an attitude. The attitude, of course, would cost extra. Caz ordered and the guy kept the smirk in place.

So Caz asked:

'What?'

The guy chuckled. It's hard to credit that a human being in this era of global terrorism would seriously make such a sound, and worse, think it was *clever*. He said:

'That's Brant you're keeping company with.'

'And that means what?'

Another chuckle, then:

'Don't let the big boys hear about that.'

Caz didn't do threats well, unless it was from Brant,

which was a whole other country. But some git in a pub?
He fingered his stiletto, said:

'I'll tell him what you said.'

And got the guy's full attention. He pleaded:

'Jesus, don't do that. Tell you what, how would it be if I
gave you these drinks as a treat from me, how would that
suit?'

It suited fine. Caz told Brant anyway. Brant was
delighted and raised his glass to the guy who busied
himself with glass-cleaning and wished he'd kept his frigging mouth shut.

Brant asked:

'Where is she?'

Caz produced a slip of paper and said:

'She's shacked up with a stripper. And Ray... Ray is in
Brighton. Both of them have changed their appearance.'

Brant was seriously impressed. He didn't show it of
course but did concede:

'Nice one.'

28

AT THE HOSPITAL, the doctor gave Andrews some painkillers after he cleaned up the bite.

He said:

'You're lucky, the woman who did this, she doesn't appear to have any... how shall I say?... condition that might raise cause for concern.'

Falls, trying to suppress the rage that still boiled, said:

'She has a condition now, all right.'

The doctor looked at her questioningly and she said:

'Assaulting a police officer, that will get her two years. You might say she'd got a fucked condition.'

The doctor was appalled at the use of language, not to mention the glee and venom of the words, and he said:

'I'm sure the poor woman needs help.'

Falls wanted to lash him, and she hated how, like Brant,

she was starting to see liberals as a serious pain in the ass. She kept the steel in her tone and asked:

'Are you married?'

He read it wrong and, flattered, conceded:

'Ahm, yes, but we've been… '

Falls cut him off with:

'And if some bitch took a chunk out of her neck, how much would your heart bleed?'

He wanted to get away and thought he might put a call through to his MP about the type of person wearing a uniform these days. He said:

'One can't, of course, predict one's reaction but one likes to believe one would weigh the factors involved.'

Andrews wanted to get out of there and stood up, but Falls added:

'Weigh this: when the bull dyke gets her biting ass in Holloway, we'll see how one might weigh that factor.'

The doctor dismissed her, said to Andrews:

'I strongly recommend you go home, get some rest. Is there anyone there to take care of you? You've had a traumatic time.'

Andrews didn't answer him and walked away. Falls gave him the long stare and followed.

He said to a nurse:

'God help us all if they're the good guys.'

29

OUTSIDE, FALLS ASKED:

'Should I call a cab?'

'I want a drink.'

Who was Falls to argue? But they were still in uniform and fairly bedraggled, so she hailed a black cab and asked him to go to Lonsdale Road. The driver had the 'Knowledge' and knew the police den there, dropped them right outside it, said:

'You guys are getting some bad press but for my money, you're doing good.'

And waived the fare.

How often does that happen? It was smart public relations but the gesture was meant.

Falls said:

'If you're ever in a jam…'

He appreciated the pun. Andrews looked at the nondescript building, asked in a sulky tone:

'What's this?'

Falls, invigorated, said:

'It's the "sorrows", as in drown the fuckers. You don't get to visit it until you've proved yourself. So many wash out now, if they last a week it's surprising but you, you've certainly shown you're here for the long haul.'

Andrews seemed singularly unimpressed but when you've recently been bitten, your options move. There were no bouncers on the door – *at a cop joint? Come on!*

A single cop sat in an alcove, reading *Loaded*, looked up and muttered:

'Falls.'

Waved them in.

You'd expect a dive and you wouldn't be more wrong. The furnishings were sedate, almost feminine, lots of fussy curtains and delicate furniture with a bright paint job. The place was jammed: uniforms, plain clothes, Special Branch, civil servants who were vaguely connected in that they did favours. A long bar running the length of one wall, and two tenders.

As they walked in, conversation stopped and then a quiet applause began. Andrews looked at Falls who said:

'That's for you, kid.'

'What? How can they know?'

Falls led the way to a corner table, acknowledged the praise with a small hand gesture and said:

'Are you joking? A cop gets hit, they know.'

Immediately a round of drinks came, and raised glasses from various tables.

Andrews asked:

'What's in these drinks?'

There were six shot glasses and Falls handed one over, said:

'Scotch, these guys are no frills.'

For a moment, it seemed like Andrews was going to demur, maybe ask for vodka and slimline tonic, but as she felt the camaraderie, something in her face changed and she knocked back the shot like a good 'un. A chorus of 'Way to go, girl' followed.

She was in.

30

PC MCDONALD HAD been hovering on the brink for days on end. His parents had come from Edinburgh and left in tears. Brant, Falls, Roberts had all made appearances. Then he came round with a massive headache.

The doctor asked:

'Are you a religious man?'

McDonald, groggy but improving, stared at him, asked:

'What?'

'A bullet creased the very top of your brain, you should be dead... at the very least, a vegetable. I've never seen such a drastic turnaround. If you're not a religious man, you better find some icon to thank because, believe you me, this is a miracle.'

McDonald didn't feel very grateful or lucky or even

miraculous; what he felt was nauseous, thirsty and a little hungry. He said so.

The doctor gave him a long look and thought: Cops, more stupid than I could have believed. He said:

'You should make a full recovery but you're going to have to take a time to rest and recuperate. Head wounds are very traumatic and all sorts of problems can arise so we'll be monitoring you.'

McDonald sighed and near whined:

'So where are we on the drink?'

The doctor stomped off and figured the worst ones always survived. He near collided with Superintendent Brown, who said:

'Hey, watch where you're going.'

The doctor saw the dog's dinner of insignia on the Super's jacket and wanted to say:

'If you're the top honcho, no wonder the idiot in the bed is so thick.'

The Super sat on the side of the bed and asked:

'How are you doing?'

McDonald managed to sit up and say:

'Bit weak but I'll be back in jig time.'

The Super snorted, which is exactly how it sounded: the noise coming down his nose full of derision and scepticism. He drew back his shoulders as his wife was always nagging him to do and barked:

'That's what you think, laddie!'

McDonald was confused; he thought the Super had come to praise him.

Before he could protest, the Super continued:

'I still have some juice despite having to eat shit over arresting the wrong suspect so I've persuaded the media to treat you as a hero cop. All that good nonsense about tackling an armed and highly dangerous villain – the great unwashed still love the good old British "have a go" shite. You'll probably get a commendation.'

He paused to let this sink in and McDonald didn't know whether to say thanks or just shut his mouth. He decided to shut his mouth.

The Super looked round and wasn't impressed with anything he saw, then:

'You'll get the commendation but that's all you'll bloody get. I had my eye on you, was even putting you up for the Lodge, but you're finished, you hear me? You went off on your own bat and nearly caused a huge disaster. I'll be covering our arse for months to come, thanks to you, and worse, we have a lunatic out there with a ton of our money and a weapon.'

Brown stood up, breathed heavily, added:

'If you do come back, you'll be on traffic, and we can only hope you don't make a complete bollix of that.'

Then he stomped off.

A nurse went over to McDonald, gave the hero her sweetest smile and asked:

'Now, love, what would you like?'

'Like? What would I like? I'd like you to fuck off!'

It took two orderlies to hold him down while they gave him a massive sedative.

31

FALLS WAS SINKING her third shot when Brant strode in. He was wearing a light blue suit, open white shirt and soft leather boots that screamed money. He pulled up a chair and asked:

'Join you, girls?'

Andrews was delighted and Falls felt her heart sink. For years, she'd struggled not to become like him but the more she did, the more she seemed to blend into him.

The cops at the bar gave him grudging waves; they were afraid not to. A round of drinks soon arrived and he gave his wolf smile. He raised one, pointed the glass at Andrews, said:

'Here's to you losing your cherry.'

Andrews picked up hers and smiled, the flirt-filled one that lets you know you're batting ten. Brant took out his cigs and didn't offer, lit up, blew the smoke in Falls' direction and said:

'We've finally got a break in the case.'

The women in unison went:

'What?'

He enjoyed the reaction, said:

'Yeah, we know where the mysterious woman is and have a line on Ray Cross, the cop shooter. I'm picking up Porter Nash and bringing him along to meet the woman.'

Falls picked up another shot. She was chilling out and wondered why she didn't get to this place more often;, the company of cops, it was the best. The budding chemistry between Andrews and Brant was vaguely worrying but what could she do? She asked:

'Porter is out?'

'Yeah, he's raring to go and he wants Cross so bad, you know how that goes?'

Falls had a moment and knew he was referring to the rumours of her offing the cop killer. She smiled – keep it light, she told herself.

Andrews, now in her element with a man in attendance (not to mention in admiration), stood up, asked:

'Get you guys a drink?'

Brant said:

'My kind of girl. Get the same again and see if they have any salt 'n' vinegar. Some nuts for Falls, she hasn't had any for ages.'

Andrews positively flounced off.

Falls said:

'Any chance you'll let this one go?'

'Who, the suspect?'

She leaned over, took one of his cigs – and you had to know him a *long* time to risk that – and said:

'Don't be coy, I mean this WPC. Could you pass on her?'

He loved it. His eyes closed for a moment, then he said:

'Gotta break 'em in, you know how it goes. Here, you want me to light that?'

And leant over.

She could smell some aftershave, just a hint but superior quality. She'd been hoping it was Old Spice or some predictable crap. She crushed his cig, dropped it on the table and he gave her the lazy look, said:

'Could cost you.'

Andrews returned with bags of crisps, drinks, said:

'Whoops, I forgot your nuts.'

Brant stood, said:

'Gotta run but here's my address. Why don't you gals come over later? We'll make some music, how would that be?'

Andrews looked at the fresh drinks, pleaded:

'But your drink?'

Brant handed over his card, said:

'You keep it warm for me, hon.'

And was gone.

Falls felt something close to jealousy and tried to bite down. She wanted to warn Andrews about Brant but knew it would only come out badly. The decision was made for her by the painkillers Andrews had received in the hospital. They kicked in and, with the series of neat whiskies, Andrews' head began to droop. Falls managed to get her address from her and called a cab.

As they left, Falls holding her by the shoulders, one of the cops shouted:

'Give her one for me.'

The cab driver asked:

'Is she going to throw up? Only I've just had the car cleaned.'

Falls showed her teeth and he shut up. Back at the address, Falls was surprised to see a tidy, two-storey house and asked Andrews for her key.

She muttered:

'Ring the doorbell.'

She did and it was thrown open by a middle-aged woman who ranted:

'What have you done to my daughter?'

Falls was too tired to do parents and said:

'She got bitten today so ease up. All right?'

The woman was having none of it:

'So you went and got her drunk. Is that modern policing?'

Andrews, meanwhile, was slumped in the doorway, whimpering. Falls tried to help her up and the woman pushed her away, shouting:

'Don't you put your black hands on my girl. I don't know what the world is coming to. She wasn't brought up to this you know; she only ever saw you people from a distance.'

Falls didn't know if she meant cops or blacks but had a good idea. She turned to go and added as a parting shot:

'Yeah, well guess what? She's been up close and personal now and I think she likes it.'

The door was slammed in her face.

'The fuck you talking about?'

'My question is, do I cut your dick off and stick it in your mouth before I shoot you...'

'Hey – hey, listen to me a minute, no shit—'

'Or do I shoot you and then cut your dick off? I always wondered,' Vincent said, 'since I'm not up on any of your quaint guinea customs yo guys're into, leaving the dead rat, any of that kind a shit. I think I know which way you'd prefer... '

Elmore Leonard, *Glitz*.

31

BRANT WAS DRIVING a Toyota Corolla he'd borrowed from a guy who owed him a favour. The guy, nervous at Brant having the car, had asked:

'You'll be careful? I mean, it's like, almost brand new.'

Brant gave him the smile, said:

'I'll treat it like a woman.'

That's what the guy was afraid of and cringed as Brant burned rubber driving away.

Porter Nash lived in Kennington, an area that – according to the posh mags at least – was coming back. Which led you to wonder, where had it been? Brant, feeling good from the encounter with Andrews, leaned on the horn until Porter appeared. He was dressed in faded jeans, police gym track-top and trainers, a light raincoat topping off the ensemble.

He asked:

'What's with the horn-blowing?'

'Get the neighbours cranked, let 'em know the boys in blue are on the job.'

Porter got in and said:

'I'm not even going to ask where you got the car.'

'Smart.'

Brant drove like a demented person, lethal turns and cutting off black cabs at every opportunity. Porter lit a cig and Brant said:

'Hey, aren't you supposed to be off those?'

'When this case is done, then I'm done.'

They pulled up at a quiet house and saw the windows were all lit up.

Brant said:

'They're home.'

He ran through what he'd learned from the snitch: that Angie had been running with Ray Cross, that Ray was in Brighton. Brant was hoping for an address on him soon. Porter digested the data then asked:

'You think she's involved?'

'Let's go find out.'

Angie opened the door, asked:

'Yes?'

They showed the warrant cards and she invited them in. Walking ahead of them, Brant took a good look at her and thought she had the moves. In the sitting room, she asked if she could perhaps get them some refreshment. They declined and she motioned them to sit. They did.

Angie was dressed like a secretary: a very low-key secretary at that. A beige suit, with a simple white blouse and low heels, a single strand of pearls around her neck. The boys weren't buying this.

The look in her eyes said:

'You believe this shit?'

They didn't.

Brant began, his notebook on his lap, as if he had to consult it. He asked:

'You were the girlfriend of Ray Cross?'

She ran her tongue along her bottom lip, feigning nervousness, answered:

'Yes, but I had to flee.'

In unison they went:

'Flee?'

Brant enjoyed the image. The idea of this babe fleeing anyone or anything just didn't gel. She folded her hands on her knees, a demure gesture and Porter thought she was close to wringing her hands.

She said:

'I was afraid of him. He had a gun and I began to suspect he was involved in dangerous activities.'

Porter felt he should join in, asked:

'And you didn't think to contact the police?'

Now the hand-wringing, with:

'Oh, he'd have found out and I don't know what he might have done.'

Brant lit a cig, then asked:

'Mind?'

'May I have one?'

He offered the pack and she took it delicately, shook one loose, waited for him to move. He reached over and fired her up.

Porter watched as she let her fingers touch Brant's, ever so fleetingly.

Brant blew out the smoke, asked:

'And the brother, Jimmy, how'd you get on with him?'

A few tears slid down her cheeks and neither offered a hankie. She sniffed, then:

'Oh, Jimmy was too good for this world. He was an innocent, I can't believe he's dead.'

Porter had been impressed with the horn-rimmed glasses she'd been wearing. She removed them now to dry her eyes. Before he could comment, they heard a moan from the bedroom, Angie tried to smile, said:

'My flatmate, she'd come down with some bug.'

Brant stood, asked:

'Mind if I see how she's doing?'

Angie, alarmed, stood, said:

'There's no need, she'll be fine, you'll only disturb her.'

Brant exchanged a look with Porter who nodded and Brant said:

'Lady, it's what I do best: disturb people.'

He marched into the bedroom and Angie began to wring her hands in earnest.

Rachel, in a tangle of sheets, was sweating like a horse, vomit on the floor. Brant bent down, asked:

'Karen?'

She managed a smile, asked:

'Brant?'

'Yeah, it's me darlin', what's going on with you?'

She explained the twisted feeling in her gut, how she'd apparently recover and then be sick all over again, that she couldn't get the smell of almonds out of her nostrils. Brant rubbed her forehead, asked:

'And Angie, lemme guess, she's been doing the meals?'

Karen struggled to sit up and croaked, said:

'Yes, she insists I eat that shite, that muesli every morning.'

Brant, who'd been poisoned himself by a Spanish psycho, said:

'We're going to get you to the hospital. You'll be fine.'

He came out, using his cellphone, saying:

'Going to need an ambulance in jig time. Yeah, suspected poisoning and send a scene-of-crime team; we're going to turn this place over.'

He looked at Porter, said:

'Miss Prim here has been feeding arsenic or cyanide to her flatmate. I can never remember which one smells like almonds.'

He levelled his gaze at Angie, said:

'You're fucked, babe.'

Porter stood and moved right in front of her, asked:

'The night Jimmy had his accident, where were you, sweetheart?'

Angie, smiling again, took another of Brant's cigs, said:

'You're going to love this.'

In unison they answered:

'Doubt it.'

Angie crossed her legs, letting them see lots of thigh, drew deep on the cig, said:

'I was with a cop.'

Took them by surprise and they said nothing. She was enjoying this, gauged their reactions to her leg display and figured the polite guy was a fag but the other, he'd ride a camel. So she directed her comments at him, said:

'I was with a cop in the biblical sense, you get my drift?'

They felt the initiative slipping away and Brant said:

'Who was he?'

He was thinking, *Fuck this, I'll kill the asshole* but tried to act like this wasn't a big deal.

Angie was daring him now and asked:

'What makes you think it was a he?'

Porter, before he could think spluttered:

'What the hell does that mean?'

Now she turned those eyes on him, said:

'I'd have thought you'd be sympathetic to same sex gigs. It was a sharp little dame named Falls. The black meat, it's always a little exotic, don't you think?'

Porter shook his head and went to see the state of Karen. Angie stared at Brant, said:

'This is no big thing. She took some shit, thought it would bring her weight down. She's a stripper, we're not talking rocket scientist so how about you let it slide? I'll give you a blow job like you've only ever dreamed about and that's just the beginning... What do you say, fellah, you think you'd go for that?'

Brant seemed as if he was considering it and her hopes rose, then he shrugged, said:

'Thing is, honey, I don't do dykes.'

32

RAY BROUGHT HIS train ticket, the gun in a holdall. The ticket clerk had asked:

'Return?'

'Not on your bloody life.'

He settled in his seat and took out a Special Brew, feeling better already at the thought of getting back to London.

A guy in a suit, reading *The Financial Times* peered over the top of the paper, said:

'Is it your intention to drink that?'

Ray gave him the look, said:

'It's my intention to come and sit with you, right up close, how would that be?'

The suit moved.

After a few cans, Ray was building a nice little buzz and

went for a pee, locked the door and as he relieved himself, he went:

'Ah.'

He checked his reflection and was shocked anew at the red hair, thinking, *Fuck, geek city*.

At Waterloo, there were lots of cops in evidence but he didn't get more than a second glance. Found a B&B in Lower Marsh and paid a week in advance.

He went out that evening, the gun in the waistband of his jeans, it felt like reassurance. He headed for a stripclub in Clapham. Had a few brewskis and waited.

He was watching a girl named Donna; she couldn't dance for shit but the punters – dazed from bad lighting, watered drinks and the seediness of the place – seemed to like her. When she took her break, he moved, joined her at her table, asked:

'What do you say to a bottle of champers?'

She was about to say *piss off* but peered closely, went:

'Ray?'

Donna had a serious nose-candy problem, the septum already in the final stages of disintegration. Her constant sniffle became irritating very fast. She wiped at her nostrils and Ray could see she was hurting. He laid a fat envelope on the table, said:

'Enough there to keep you in blow for a month.'

Her hand reached out and he grabbed her wrist, asked:

'Where's Angie?'

'You wouldn't hurt her or anything, would you, Ray?'

'Hey, Donna, she's my old lady; I just want to get some readies to her.'

Donna couldn't take her eyes off the envelope, tried hard and said:

'I could deliver it for you.'

Now she got his smile and it wasn't any relation of warmth. He tightened his grip on her wrist, said:

'Not that I don't trust you, doll, but I'd like to surprise her. You can understand that.'

She gave him Karen's address and cautioned:

'They're looking everywhere for you. The filth say there's good will for whoever gives you up.'

He leaned closer, whispered:

'I've some nasty friends, anything happens to me, they come visit you, get my meaning?'

She attempted to act offended, said:

'Jeez, Ray, you think I'd sell you out?'

He stood up and released her wrist, shoved the envelope across the table and said:

'Blow hard.'

He was moving away from the table when she said:

'Hey, what about the champagne?'

He laughed out loud.

And got to the place in time to see police and the ambulance, and Angie being shoved into the back of a cop car.

He said:

'Ah girl, what have you been at now?'

He wasn't unduly worried. If he knew his woman as well as he suspected, she'd be out on bail in no time.

33

ANGIE HAD BEEN allowed her call and got hold of Ellen Dunne, the radical lawyer who liked nothing better than to bust the cops' balls. As Angie sat in the interrogation room, Porter Nash said:

'Do yourself a favour, spill the beans and we can cut you some slack.'

Angie yawned, said:

'Fuck off.'

Outside the room, Roberts was listening to Brant's account and asked:

'Did you have a warrant, anything remotely like just cause or some frigging legal basis?'

Brant was offended, lit a cig and spat:

'She's dirty; at the very least we can have her for poisoning her mate.'

Roberts shook his head, said:

'Look at her, she seem like she's worried? She'll claim the woman was self-administering. Strippers, they take all kinds of shit to clear their complexions, keep their weight down and, besides, she's got the best defence. Why would she do it? The woman was helping her out: it doesn't make sense and a judge would more than likely throw it out. Here's Falls, she's really fucked up this time.'

Falls was the worse for wear and when she heard Angie was using her as alibi, she felt her whole world collapse. Roberts came at her like a Rottweiler, demanding:

'Tell me you weren't with this Angie on the night Jimmy Cross got hot-wired.'

Falls looked to Brant for some signal but he was leaning against the wall, his eyes hard. She said:

'I'm so sorry, sir.'

He exploded, his hands clenched, roared:

'Jesus H Christ, how many times have Brant and I saved your ass, gone to bat for you against all the odds, how many bloody times?'

Before she could form a reply, he turned and went into the interview room. Brant lit a cig, blew smoke at the ceiling, said:

'Me? I don't give a toss what people do – shag sheep, who cares? And to tell you the truth, a little lezzie action, I can appreciate that, it's so French. But fucking the enemy, that's screwing the job, and without that, we're really screwed, so if I were you, lady, I'd check the wanted ads for security guard placements.'

He pushed off from the wall and with, a rough gesture, ground the cig beneath his boot. Falls, who'd had to enlist his help so many times, felt total despair.

She tried:

'Maybe the time-frame will help. Maybe she came to me after Jimmy got fried. Can we get the time of death?'

She knew how poor this was but hey, she was sinking and fas,t but had to try. He gave her the stare of total disinterest, the worst thing he could have done. In their time, he'd fixed those granite eyes on her with everything from hate to lust, amusement to disappointment and even on odd moments, pride, but never this. He said:

'You'd have been drinking so how reliable are you? I'd pegged you for a lot of stuff, Falls, but a dyke, never.'

At that, the doors swung open and a heavy-set woman came striding in. Ellen Dunne, the darling of the Left and the scourge of the Met, looking something like an over-weight Glenda Jackson. She had been courted by various parties but a political career would never be the fun that busting cops was. She was waving a newspaper and, fixing her gaze on Brant, said:

'See the headline?'

Brant set his wolf smile, answered:

'You know me,Ellen, I'm a pig. Would I have the sense to read papers?'

'Let me read it for you, it's so "up your street"… listen: "I'd like to say to all international drug dealers, if you'd be so kind as to stand up against that wall for a moment… Then I'd shout: 'Ready, aim, fire!'."'

Brant shrugged and Ellen said:

'This isn't a tabloid hack but something written by Chief Constable Terry Grange. Is this your boys in blue? Where's my client?'

Brant nodded towards the interview room and she pushed past.

Angie was sipping from a Diet Coke, Roberts standing near the window, Porter sitting opposite Angie.

Ellen gave them her gallows smile, said:

'Might I have a moment to confer with my client?'

They moved to leave and Ellen looked closer at Porter, asked:

'Hey, aren't you Porter Nash?'

He stopped, said:

'So?'

She studied him, then:

'The fag? We were hoping you'd bring some light into this abyss but... You're over-compensating. Think that if you're more of a fascist than the rest of them, they'll let you be one of the lads? Is that it?'

Porter was stung and snapped:

'I expected more of you, Ms Dunne.'

Angie was enjoying this and delighted that Dunne was even better than she'd heard, said:

'He wanted me to cop a plea.'

Ellen was still studying him, asked:

'Didn't you have a heart attack or something?'

Porter wanted to lash out, come up with some scathing put-down, but all he had was:

'Like you care?'

Ellen turned to sit down, said:

'I don't.'

Twenty minutes later, Angie was cut loose and Ellen threatened:

'We'll sue your asses off.'

The assembled group – Brant, Falls, Roberts, steeped in their respective misery – were silent. Porter had disappeared.

After Angie had gone, Ellen's arm protectively round her shoulder, Roberts turned to Falls, said:

'Go home, you're a complete liability. No doubt you'll be bounced as soon as the hearing is done *and* you're suspended without pay, got it?'

As Falls left the building, the desk sergeant whispered:

'You let guys watch when you're doing chicks? I could line up some gigs.'

She was too wretched to give him the finger.

Angie had gone to the pub, bought Ellen a large brandy and a vodka for herself.

Ellen cautioned:

'Watch your step now. Those bastards have been badly humiliated, they'll do anything to get you. Have you a place to stay?'

Angie, feeling powerful, adrenaline coursing through her, said:

'I'm going home.'

'Where's home?'

'The Mews, where I lived with Ray and his late brother.'

Ellen knocked back the brandy, took a deep breath, asked:

'Is that wise? I mean, until they catch Ray.'

Angie was already thinking of the money and how it was time to get out, smiled, said:

'Ray is a punk, hasn't the bottle to return to London; he'll be skulking in some hole till they come and waste his shit.'

They had another few drinks and Angie explained how, if Karen was to receive a few quid, she'd readily cop to have taken the poison herself. Ellen, watching Angie as she went through this, began to feel a chill.

In her thirty years of law, she'd encountered all kinds, some of the supposedly most dangerous people in the country and she'd never felt afraid, but now, as the essence of this woman began to permeate her senses, she felt a growing fear, a downright feeling that here was the real thing. Here was the so-called evil that psychologists claimed didn't really exist.

Angie, in her elation, had let her true self emerge, her eyes no longer guarded, and what looked out was as old as time and primeval in its malevolence. Ellen had, without realising it, moved a few feet away, a voice in her head urging her to get the hell out of there. Angie, always sensitive to danger, put out her hand, touched Ellen's wrist, asked:

'You okay? You don't look too good.'

'The brandy. I'm not used to it on an empty stomach.'

She got up, left fast and felt she had indeed supped with the devil. She'd relegate this case to a junior.

The old man was up from his chair and looking at
Len with hot eyes.
'You want to smack the shit out of me and end this?' He
said. 'I wouldn't even hit you back.'
Len sat at the table and watched his father put his hands
in his back pockets and stand
a minute as if something wild.
*You're not the man I was shit scared of. You can't even
stand up against a wind anymore.*
Daniel Buckman, *The Name of Rivers*.

34

ANGIE WENT TO the lock-up off Clapham Common first, failed to notice the various people following her. Inside, she packed the money into a suitcase and put her Browning automatic into her handbag. She had a passport and reckoned she was ready to roll. A fast visit to the Mews and she'd get ready to split.

She was feeling better than she ever had done, fooled 'em all and got to stick it in their faces. The only minor flaw was Ray having the other half of the money, but maybe she'd get lucky and find some clue to its where-abouts at the Mews. Ray wasn't the brightest and wouldn't have exactly found a brilliant hiding place.

She got to the Mews by cab and enjoyed the cabbie trying to hit on her.

He said:

'Honey, you look like a woman who's got it all.'

She laughed and thought how right he was. The Mews was cold and in a mess. The cops had tossed it pretty good. She got some coffee going then added a little scotch, warm her up. She kicked off her shoes and had barely taken a sip when the key went in the door and a ginger-haired guy walked in.

She did a double take and then:

'Ray?'

He smiled, said:

'You got me, babe.'

She looked at her handbag, the Browning inside it. Ray caught the look, said:

'Got a little protection in there?'

And took the .38 out of his jacket, levelled it, said:

'Killing Jimmy, was that necessary?'

He shot her in the stomach and heard a voice say:

'Drop the gun, shithead.'

Two cops came out of the bedroom. One looked ill, as if he'd recently been in hospital, the other looked like a hard fuck. They both had guns pointing at him. Ray tried to bring his round and the hard ass shot him in the head.

Porter Nash said:

'Jeez, Brant, did you have to do that?'

'Yeah. Yeah, I did.'

Angie was moaning and Porter Nash got on the phone. Brant checked Ray was dead and then moved to Angie, said:

'I'll bet that hurts.'

She tried to spit but the pain was too great. She managed:

'You executed him. I'll tell my brief.'

Brant opened the suitcase, said:

'Tell her about the extortion money, too. She'll be interested in that.'

The ambulance took her away, handcuffed to the gurney. Porter Nash went along and she managed to call him various obscenities. He felt tired and his chest was paining him.

Brant was in the pub, downing doubles. The shot he'd fired was still amazing him. He'd meant to hit the fuck in the knee, to enable them to find out where the rest of the money was at. As he drained his drink, he relived the moment and said:

'Like they say, there ain't no coming back from a head wound.'

The barman, eyeing Brant's glass, asked:

'Another shot?'

Brant laughed out loud, said:

'Nope, just needed the one.'

35

WHEN THE EXCITEMENT died down and the various cops had moved away, Falls moved from her vigil. Shit, she was cold, had been standing under the trees opposite the Mews for hours. Had trailed Angie from the lock-up, watched her enter the house, then had been confused by a red-haired guy who followed shortly after… unsure as to what to do, she'd waited until she'd heard the shots, then she'd rushed over. Through a window she'd seen Brant and Porter, on top of the situation, if two bodies classed as 'being on top'. Then she'd waited for hours as the ambulance came and a shitpile of blue.

Her mind asking:

'What are you waiting for?'

She didn't know.

When it had all settled down, she finally moved and

broke in through a back window. She could see the blood on the floor and the mess from the many feet that had trampled around.

A bottle of scotch was left on the table, half full. She tilted it and drank deep. There was very little to see and she decided to head home but then, a picture on the far wall caught her eye. She inspected it and recognised it as a vixen. Was it her jittery state or did the animal have some resemblance to Angie? Whatever, she took it, let it be a scold to how she'd fucked up.

Hailed a cab and got home in the hour before dawn, the cabbie saying:

'Late to be out, ma'am.'

Ma'am! Jesus, how old was that?

Inside, she had a shower and changed into her old cotton pyjamas, the ones with the false scent of homeliness. Got another big drink going and decided to try and hang the picture but hell, it weighed a ton. She turned it over and the back was literally packed solid: how distracted had she been that she hadn't noticed already? Got a knife and began to hack at the filling until packets of money began to tumble out. The more she hacked, the more money flowed. She began to laugh, thinking Roberts had suspended her without pay... she flung wedges of money in the air, shouting:

'Fuck 'em if they can't take a joke.'

36

A WEEK LATER, PC McDonald was home, lying on the sofa, sunk in deep depression, thinking: If I could only get away, I could maybe get some perspective. The post came and among the bills was a padded envelope. He opened it without interest and to his disbelief, saw thick piles of money. A single sheet of paper contained the typed sentence:

'You're a fox.'

He got the telephone directory, began to look up travel agencies.

37

IN HOLLOWAY PRISON, Beth, a prisoner recently blinded by bad home-made hooch, was trying to roll a cigarette. A voice said:

'Let me get that for you?'

She did.

Then the cig was put between her lips and the voice asked:

'So, you got any more perfect crimes?'

Ken Bruen

hails from Galway in the west of Ireland, where he currently lives with his wife and daughter. His past includes twenty-five years as an English teacher in Africa, Japan, south-east Asia and South America, a PhD in metaphysics and some of the most acclaimed novels of our time. 'Vixen' is his fifteenth book and follows on from the 'White' Trilogy (*A White Arrest*, *Taming The Alien* and *The McDead*) and the subsequent *Blitz*.

Also published by THE DO-NOT PRESS

Grief by John B Spencer
'*Grief* is a speed-freak's cocktail, one part Leonard and one part Ellroy,
that goes right to the head.' George P Pelecanos
When disparate individuals collide, it's Grief. John B Spencer's
final and greatest novel.
'Spencer writes the tightest dialogue this side of Elmore Leonard, so
bring on the blood, sweat and beers!' Ian Rankin

No One Gets Hurt by Russell James
'The best of Britain's darker crime writers' – *The Times*
After a friend's murder Kirsty Rice finds herself drawn into the
murky world of call-girls, porn and Internet sex.

Kiss It Away by Carol Anne Davis
'Reminiscent of Ruth Rendell at her darkest' – Booklist (USA)
Steroid dependent Nick arrives alone in Salisbury, rapes a stranger
and brutally murders a woman.
'A gripping tale of skewered psychology… a mighty chiller,'
The Guardian

A Man's Enemies by Bill James
'Bill James can write, and then some' *The Guardian*
The direct sequel to 'Split'. Simon Abelard, the section's 'token black',
has to dissuade Horton from publishing his memoirs.

End of the Line by K T McCaffrey
'KT McCaffrey is an Irish writer to watch' RTE
Emma is celebrating her Journalist of the Year Award when she hears
of the death of priest Father Jack O'Gorman in what appears to have
been a tragic road accident.

Green for Danger edited by Martin Edwards
THE OFFICIAL CWA ANTHOLOGY 2004
A brand new and delicious selection of the best modern crime
writing themed on 'crime in the countryside'.
The 20 contributors include: Andrea Badenoch, Robert Barnard,
Carol Anne Davis, Martin Edwards, Reginald Hill, Michael Jecks,
Peter Lovesey and Ruth Rendell.

The Do-Not Press
Fiercely Independent Publishing

Keep in touch with what's happening at the cutting edge of independent British publishing.

Simply send your name and address to:
The Do-Not Press (VIXEN)
16 The Woodlands, London SE13 6TY (UK)

or email us: vixen@thedonotpress.com

There is no obligation to purchase
(although we'd certainly like you to!)
and no salesman will call.

Visit our regularly-updated websites:

www.thedonotpress.com
www.bangbangbooks.com

Mail Order

All our titles are available from good bookshops, or (in case of difficulty) direct from The Do-Not Press at the address above. There is no charge for post and packing for orders to the UK and Europe.

(NB: A post-person may call.)